THE GLENCOE LITERATURE LIBRARY

Shiloh

and Related Readings

Glencoe
McGraw-Hill

New York, New York   Columbus, Ohio   Woodland Hills, California   Peoria, Illinois

Acknowledgments

Grateful acknowledgment is given authors, publishers, photographers, museums, and agents for permission to reprint the following copyrighted material. Every effort has been made to determine copyright owners. In case of any omissions, the Publisher will be pleased to make suitable acknowledgments in future editions.

SHILOH by Phyllis Reynolds Naylor. Copyright © 1991 by Phyllis Reynolds Naylor. All rights reserved. This edition is reprinted by arrangement with Atheneum Books for Young Readers, Simon & Schuster Children's Publishing Division.

"The Christmas Fake" by Lois Lenski, from LOIS LENSKI'S CHRISTMAS STORIES. Copyright © 1968 by Lois Lenski. Reprinted by permission of HarperCollns Publisher.

From STRIDE TOWARD FREEDOM by Martin Luther King, Jr. Copyright © 1963 by Martin Luther King, Jr., copyright renewed 1991 by Coretta Scott King. Reprinted by arrangement with The Heirs to the Estate of Martin Luther King, Jr., c/o Writers House, Inc. as agents for the proprietor.

"What Ever Became of Honest Abe" by Ezra Bowen, from TIME April 4, 1988, copyright © 1988 TIME INC. Reprinted by permission.

"Stray" by Cynthia Rylant reprinted with the permission of Simon & Schuster Books for Young Readers, an imprint of Simon & Schuster Children's Publishing Division. From EVERY LIVING THING by Cynthia Rylant. Copyright © 1985 Cynthia Rylant.

"The Bell of Atri" from FAIR IS FAIR: World Folktales of Justice by Sharon Creeden. Copyright © 1994 Sharon Creeden. Published by August House Publishers, Inc. and reprinted with their permission.

Cover Art: "A *Hound*, Anonymous," Private Collection/Bridgeman Art Library

Glencoe/McGraw-Hill

A Division of The **McGraw·Hill** Companies

Send all inquiries to:
Glencoe/McGraw-Hill
8787 Orion Place
Columbus, OH 43240

ISBN 0-07-820371-6
Printed in the United States of America
8 9 10 11 12 DOC 13 12 11 10

Contents

Shiloh

Continued

Contents *continued*

Shiloh

Phyllis Reynolds Naylor

Chapter 1

THE DAY SHILOH COME, we're having us a big Sunday dinner. Dara Lynn's dipping bread in her glass of cold tea, the way she likes, and Becky pushes her beans up over the edge of her plate in her rush to get 'em down.

Ma gives us her scolding look. "Just once in my life," she says, "I'd like to see a bite of food go direct from the dish into somebody's mouth without a detour of any kind."

She's looking at me when she says it, though. It isn't that I don't like fried rabbit. Like it fine. I just don't want to bite down on buckshot, is all, and I'm checking each piece.

"I looked that rabbit over good, Marty, and you won't find any buckshot in that thigh," Dad says, buttering his bread. "I shot him in the neck."

Somehow I wish he hadn't said that. I push the meat from one side of my plate to the other, through the sweet potatoes and back again.

"Did it die right off?" I ask, knowing I can't eat at all unless it had.

"Soon enough."

"You shoot its head clean off?" Dara Lynn asks. She's like that.

Dad chews real slow before he answers. "Not quite," he says, and goes on eating.

Which is when I leave the table.

The best thing about Sundays is we eat our big meal at noon. Once you get your belly full, you can walk all over West Virginia before you're hungry again. Any other day, you start out after dinner, you've got to come back when it's dark.

I take the .22 rifle Dad had given me in March on my eleventh birthday and set out up the road to see what I can shoot. Like to find me an apple hanging way out on a branch, see if I can bring it down. Line up a few cans on a rail fence and shoot 'em off. Never shoot at anything moving, though. Never had the slightest wish.

We live high up in the hills above Friendly, but hardly anybody knows where that is. Friendly's near Sistersville, which is halfway between Wheeling and Parkersburg. Used to be, my daddy told me, Sistersville was one of the best places you could live in the whole state. You ask *me* the best place to live, I'd say right where we are, a little four-room house with hills on three sides.

Afternoon is my second-best time to go up in the hills, though; morning's the best, especially in summer. Early, *early* morning. On one morning I saw three kinds of animals, not counting cats, dogs, frogs, cows, and horses. Saw a groundhog, saw a doe with two fawns, and saw a gray fox with a reddish head. Bet his daddy was a gray fox and his ma was a red one.

My favorite place to walk is just across this rattly bridge where the road curves by the old Shiloh schoolhouse and follows the river. River to one side, trees the other—sometimes a house or two.

And this particular afternoon, I'm about halfway up the road along the river when I see something out of the corner of my eye. Something moves. I look, and about fifteen yards off, there's this shorthaired dog—white with brown and black spots-not making any kind of noise, just slinking along with his head down, watching me, tail between his legs like he's hardly got the right to breathe. A beagle, maybe a year or two old.

I stop and the dog stops. Looks like he's been caught doing something awful, when I can tell all he really wants is to follow along beside me.

"Here, boy," I say, slapping my thigh.

Dog goes down on his stomach, groveling about in the grass. I laugh and start over toward him. He's got an old worn-out collar on, probably older than he is. Bet it belonged to another dog before him. "C'mon, boy," I say, putting out my hand.

The dog gets up and backs off. He don't even whimper, like he's lost his bark.

Something really hurts inside you when you see a dog cringe like that. You know somebody's been kicking him. Beating on him, maybe.

"It's okay, boy," I'll say, coming a little closer, but still he backs off.

So I just take my gun and follow the river. Every so often I look over my shoulder and there he is, the beagle. I stop; he stops. I can see his ribs—not real bad—but he isn't plumped out or anything.

There's a broken branch hanging from a limb out over the water, and I'm wondering if I can bring it down with one shot. I raise my gun, and then I think how the sound might scare the dog off. I decide I don't want to shoot my gun much that day.

It's a slow river. You walk beside it, you figure it's not even moving. If you stop, though, you can see leaves and things going along. Now and then a fish jumps—big fish. Bass, I think. Dog's still trailing me, tail tucked in. Funny how he don't make a sound.

Finally I sit on a log, put my gun at my feet, and wait. Back down the road, the dog sits, too. Sits right in the middle of it, head on his paws.

"Here, boy!" I say again, and pat my knee.

He wiggles just a little, but he don't come.

Maybe it's a she-dog.

"Here, girl!" I say. Dog still don't come.

I decide to wait the dog out, but after three or four minutes on the log, it gets boring and I start off again. So does the beagle.

Don't know where you'd end up if you followed the river all the way. Heard somebody say it curves about, comes back on itself, but if it didn't and I got home after dark, I'd get a good whopping. So I always go as far as the ford, where the river spills across the path, and then I head back.

When I turn around and the dog sees me coming, he goes off into the woods. I figure that's the last I'll see of the beagle, and I get halfway down the road again before I look back. There he is. I stop. He stops. I go. He goes.

And then, hardly thinking on it, I whistle.

It's like pressing a magic button. The beagle comes barreling toward me, legs going lickety-split, long ears flopping, tail sticking up like a flagpole. This time, when I put out my hand, he licks all my fingers and jumps up against my leg, making little yelps in his throat. He can't get enough of me, like I'd been saying no all along and now I'd said yes, he could come. It's a he-dog, like I'd thought.

"Hey, boy! You're really somethin' now, ain't you?" I'm laughing as the beagle makes circles around me. I squat down and the dog licks my face, my neck. Where'd he learn to come if you whistled, to hang back if you didn't?

I'm so busy watching the dog I don't even notice it's started to rain. Don't bother me. Don't bother the dog, neither. I'm looking for the place I first saw him. Does he live here? I wonder. Or the house on up the road? Each place we pass I figure he'll stop—somebody come out and whistle, maybe. But nobody comes out and the dog don't stop. Keeps coming even after we get to the old Shiloh schoolhouse. Even starts across the bridge, tail going like a propeller. He licks my hand every so often to make sure I'm still there—mouth open like he's smiling. He *is* smiling.

Once he follows me across the bridge, though, and on past the gristmill, I start to worry. Looks like he's fixing to follow me all the way to our house. I'm in trouble enough coming home with my clothes wet. My ma's mama died of pneumonia, and we don't ever get the chance to forget it. And now I got a dog with me, and we were never allowed to have pets.

If you can't afford to feed 'em and take 'em to the vet when they're sick, you've no right taking 'em in, Ma says, which is true enough.

I don't say a word to the beagle the rest of the way home, hoping he'll turn at some point and go back. The dog keeps coming.

I get to the front stoop and say, "Go home, boy." And then I feel my heart squeeze up the way he stops smiling, sticks his tail between his legs again, and slinks off. He goes as far as the sycamore tree, lies down in the wet grass, head on his paws.

"Whose dog is that?" Ma asks when I come in.

I shrug. "Just followed me, is all."

"Where'd it pick up with you?" Dad asks.

"Up in Shiloh, across the bridge," I say.

"On the road by the river? Bet that's Judd Travers's beagle," says Dad. "He got himself another hunting dog a few weeks back."

"Judd got him a hunting dog, how come he don't treat him right?" I ask.

"How you know he don't?"

"Way the dog acts. Scared to pee, almost," I say.

Ma gives me a look.

"Don't seem to me he's got any marks on him," Dad says, studying him from our window.

Don't have to mark a dog to hurt him, I'm thinking.

"Just don't pay him any attention and he'll go away," Dad says.

"And get out of those wet clothes," Ma tells me. "You want to follow your grandma Slater to the grave?"

I change clothes, then sit down and turn on the TV, which only has two channels. On Sunday afternoons, it's preaching and baseball. I watch baseball for an hour. Then I get up and sneak to the window. Ma knows what I'm about.

"That Shiloh dog still out there?" she asks.

I nod. He's looking at me. He sees me there at the window and his tail starts to thump. I name him Shiloh.

Chapter 2

SUNDAY-NIGHT SUPPER is whatever's left from noon. If nothing's left over, Ma takes cold cornmeal mush, fries up big slabs, and we eat it with Karo syrup. But this night there's still rabbit. I don't want any, but I know Shiloh does.

I wonder how long I can keep pushing that piece of rabbit around my plate. Not very long, I discover.

"You going to eat that meat, or you just playing with it?" Dad asks. "If you don't want it, I'll take it for lunch tomorrow."

"I'll eat it," I say.

"Don't you be giving it to that dog," says Ma.

I take a tiny bite.

"What's the doggy going to *eat*, then?" asks Becky. She's three, which is four years younger than Dara Lynn.

"Nothing here, that's what," says Ma.

Becky and Dara Lynn look at Dad. Now I had *them* feeling sorry for the beagle, too. Sometimes girl-children get what they want easier than I do. But not this time.

"Dog's going right back across the river when we get through eating," says Dad. "If that's Judd's new dog, he probably don't have sense enough yet to find his way home again. We'll put him in the Jeep and drive him over."

Don't know what else I figured Dad to say. Do I really think he's going to tell me to wait till morning, and if the beagle's still here, we can keep him? I try all kinds of ways to figure how I could get that rabbit meat off my plate and into my pocket, but Ma's watching every move I make.

So I excuse myself and go outside and over to the chicken coop. It's off toward the back where Ma can't see. We keep three hens, and I take one of the two eggs that was in a nest and carry it out behind the bushes.

I whistle softly. Shiloh comes loping toward me. I crack the egg and empty it out in my hands. Hold my hands down low and Shiloh eats the egg, licking my hands clean afterward, then curling his tongue down between any fingers to get every little bit.

"Good boy, Shiloh," I whisper, and stroke him all over.

I hear the back screen slam, and Dad comes out on the stoop. "Marty?"

"Yeah?" I go around, Shiloh at my heels.

"Let's take that dog home now." Dad goes over and opens the door of the Jeep. Shiloh puts his tail between his legs and just stands there, so I go around to the other side, get in, and whistle. Shiloh leaps up onto my lap, but he don't look too happy about it.

For the first time I have my arms around him. He feels warm, and when I stroke him, I can feel places on his body where he has ticks.

"Dog has ticks," I tell my dad.

"Judd'll take 'em off," Dad says.

"What if he don't?"

"It's his concern, Marty, not yours. It's not your dog. You keep to your own business."

I press myself against the back of the seat as we start down our bumpy dirt driveway toward the road. "I want to be a vet someday," I tell my dad.

"Hmm," he says.

"I want to be a traveling vet. The kind that has his office in a van and goes around to people's homes, don't make folks come to him. Read about it in a magazine at school."

"You know what you have to do to be a vet?" Dad asks.

"Got to got to school. I know that."

"You've got to have college training. Like a doctor, almost. Takes a lot of money to go to veterinary school."

My dream sort of leaks out like water in a paper bag. "I could be a veterinarian's helper," I suggest, my second choice.

"You maybe could," says Dad, and points the Jeep up the road into the hills.

Dusk is settling in now. Still warm, though. A warm July night. Trees look dark against the red sky; lights coming on in a house here, another one there. I'm thinking how in any one of these houses there's probably somebody who would take better care of Shiloh than Judd Travers would. How come this dog had to be his?

The reason I don't like Judd Travers is a whole lot of reasons, not the least is that I was in the corner store once down in Friendly and saw Judd cheat Mr. Wallace at the cash register. Judd gives the man a ten and gets him to talking, then—when Mr. Wallace gives him change—says he give him a twenty.

I blink, like I can't believe Judd done that, and old Mr. Wallace is all confused. So I say, "No I think he give you a ten."

Judd glares at me, whips out his wallet, and waves a twenty-dollar bill in front of my eye. "Whose picture's on this bill, boy?" he says.

"I don't know."

He gives me a look says, I thought so. "That's Andrew Jackson," he says. "I had two of 'em in my wallet when I walked in here, and now I only got one. This here man's got the other, and I want my change."

Mr. Wallace, he's so flustered he just digs in his money drawer and gives Judd change for a twenty, and afterward I thought what did Andrew Jackson have to do with it? Judd's so fast-talking he can get away with anything. Don't know anybody who likes him much, but around here folks keep to their own business, like Dad says. In Tyler County that's important. Way it's always been, anyhow.

Another reason I don't like Judd Travers is he spits tobacco out the corner of his mouth, and if he don't like you—and he sure don't like me—he sees just how close he can spit to where you're standing. Third reason I don't like him is because he was at the fairgrounds last year same day we were, and seemed like everyplace I was, he was in front of me, blocking my view. Standin' in front of me at the mud bog, sittin' in front of me at the tractor pull, and risin' right up out of his seat at the Jorden Globe of Death Motorcycle Act so's I missed the best part.

Fourth reason I don't like him is because he kills deer out of season. He says he don't, but I seen him once just about dusk with a young buck strapped over the hood of his truck. He tells me the buck run in front of him on the road and he accidentally run over it, but I saw the bullet hole myself. If he got caught, he'd have to pay two hundred dollars, more than he's got in the bank, I'll bet.

We're in Shiloh, now. Dad's crossing the bridge by the old abandoned gristmill, turning at the boarded-up school, and for the first time I can feel Shiloh's body begin to shake. He's trembling all over. I swallow. Try to say something to my dad and have to swallow again.

"How do you go about reporting someone who don't take care of his dog right?" I ask finally.

"Who you fixing to report, Marty?"

"Judd."

"If this dog's mistreated, he's only about one out of fifty thousand animals that is," Dad says. "Folks even bring 'em up here in the hills and let 'em out, figure they can live on rats and rabbits. Wouldn't be the first dog that wasn't treated right."

"But this one come to me to help him!" I insist. "*Knew* that's why he was following me. I got hooked on him, Dad, and I want to know he's treated right."

For the first time I can tell Dad's getting impatient with me. "Now you get that out of your head right now. If it's Travers's dog, it's no mind of ours *how* he treats it."

"What if it was a child?" I ask him, getting too smart for my own good. "If some kid was shaking like this dog is shaking you wouldn't feel no pull for keeping an eye on him?"

"Marty," Dad says, and now his voice is just plumb tired. "This here's a dog, not a child, and it's not our dog. I want you to quit going on about it. Hear?"

I shut up then. Let my hands run over Shiloh's body like maybe everywhere I touch I can protect him somehow. We're getting closer to the trailer where Judd lives with his other dogs, and already they're barking up a storm, hearing Dad's Jeep come up the road.

Dad pulls over. "You want to let him out?" he says.

I shake my head hard. "I'm not lettin' him out here till I know for sure he belongs to Judd." I'm asking for a slap in the face, but Dad don't say anything, just gets out and goes up the boards Judd has laid out in place of a sidewalk.

Judd's at the door of his trailer already, in his undershirt, peering out.

"Looks like Ray Preston," he says, through he screen.

"How you doin', Judd?"

Judd comes out on the little porch he's built at the side of his trailer, and they stand there and talk awhile. Up here in the hills you hardly ever get down to business right off. First you say your howdys and then you talk about anything else but what you come for, and finally, when the mosquitoes start to bite, you say what's on your mind. But you always edge into it, not to offend.

I can hear little bits and pieces floating out over the yard. The rain . . . the trunk . . . the tomatoes . . . the price of gasoline, and all the while Shiloh lays low in my lap, tail between his legs, shaking like a window blind in a breeze.

And then, the awful words: "Say, Judd, my boy was up here along the river this afternoon, and a beagle followed him home. Don't have any tags on his collar, but I'm remembering you got yourself another hunting dog, and wondered if he might be yours."

I'm thinking this is a bad mistake. Maybe it isn't Judd's at all, and he's such a liar he'd say it was, just to get himself still another animal to be mean to.

Judd hardly let him finish: starts off across the muddy yards in his boots. "Sure as hell bet it is," he says. "Can't keep that coon dog home to save my soul. Every time I take him hunting, he runs off before I'm through. I been out all day with the dogs, and they all come back but him."

I can hear Judd's heavy footsteps coming around the side of the Jeep, and I can smell his chewing tobacco, strong as coffee.

"Yep," he says, thrusting his face in the open window. "That's him, all right." He opens the door. "*Git* on down here!" he says, and before I can even give the dog one last pat, Shiloh leaps off my lap onto the ground and connects with Judd's right foot. He yelps and rushes off behind the trailer, tail tucked down, belly to the ground. All Judd's dogs chained out back bark like crazy.

I jump out of the Jeep too. "Please don't kick him like that," I say. "Some dogs just like to run."

"He runs all over creation," Judd says. I can tell he's studying me in the dark, trying to figure what's it to me.

"I'll keep an eye out for him," I say. "Anytime I see him away from home, I'll bring him back. I promise. Just don't kick him."

Judd only growls. "He could be a fine huntin' dog, but he tries my patience. I'll leave him be tonight, but he wanders off again, I'll whup the daylights out of him. Guarantee you that."

I swallow and swallow, and all the way home I can't speak a word, trying to hold the tears back.

Chapter 3

I DON'T SLEEP more than a couple hours that night. When I do, I dream of Shiloh. When I don't, I'm thinking about him out in the rain all afternoon, head on his paws, watching our door. Thinking how I'd disappointed him, whistling like I meant something that first time, gettin' him to come to me, then taking him on back to Judd Travers to be kicked all over again.

By five o'clock, when it's growing light, I know pretty much what I have to do: I have to buy that dog from Judd Travers.

I don't let my mind go any further; don't dwell on what Judd would want for Shiloh, or even whether he'd sell. Especially don't ask myself how I'm supposed to get the money. All I know is that I can think of only one way to get that dog away from Judd, and that's what I'm going to have to do.

My bed is the couch in the living room, so when Dad comes in to fix his breakfast, I pull on my jeans and go out to sit across from him in the kitchen. First he makes himself a lunch to carry to work. He drives his Jeep to the post office in Sistersville, where he cases mail for around two hundred families and delivers it, then comes back to the Friendly post office where he cases mail for two hundred more. Delivers that, too. Route takes him 'bout eighty-five miles on roads you can hardly git by on in winter.

" 'Mornin,' " he says to me as he stuffs a sandwich in a sack, then starts in on his breakfast, which is Wheat Chex and any fruit he can get from our peach tree. He makes himself coffee and eats the cornbread or biscuits Ma saves for him from our meal the night before.

"Can you think of a way I could earn myself some money?" I ask him, with this froggy kind of voice that shows you aren't woke up yet.

Dad takes another bite of cornbread, looks at me for a moment, then goes on studying his cereal. Says exactly what I figure he'd say: "Collect some bottles, take 'em in for deposit. Pick up some aluminum cans, maybe, for the recycling place."

"I mean real money. Got to have it faster than that."

"How fast?"

I try to think. Wish I could earn it in a week, but know I can't. Have to go out every day for a whole summer collecting cans and bottles to have much of anything at all.

"A month, maybe," I tell him.

"I'll ask along my mail route, but don't know many folks with money to spare," he says. Which is what I thought.

After Dad's gone off, Becky gets up before Ma, and I fix her a bowl of Cheerios, put her sneakers on so she won't stub her toes, and brush the snarls from her hair.

Read once in a book about how some kids earned money baby-sitting. Boy, if *I* ever got paid even a nickel for every time I've taken care of Becky—Dara Lynn, too—I'd have a lot of dollars. I do a whole bunch of jobs that other kids, other places, get paid to do, but it wouldn't ever occur to me to ask for pay. If I asked Dad, he'd say, "You live in this house, boy?" And when I'd say yes, he'd say, "Then you do your share like the rest of us."

Which is why I never asked.

"More Cheerios," says Becky, and all the while I'm making her breakfast, I'm thinking the best route to take to find aluminum cans. By the time Dara Lynn gets up, wearing one of Dad's old T-shirts for her nightgown, I'd figured how I could double my can count. But when Ma gets up a few minutes later, she takes one look at me and guesses what I'm thinking.

"You got that dog on your mind," she says, lifting the big iron skillet to the stove top and laying some bacon in it.

"Thinking don't cost nothing," I tell her.

She just gives me a little smile then and sets about making my bacon crisp, the way I like it, and we don't say any more about Judd's dog.

Must walk five miles that morning, and all I find is seven cans and one bottle. When Dad comes home about four, he hasn't found anybody looking for help, either, but he says, "The Sears fall catalog come in this afternoon, Marty. You got nothing better to do tomorrow, you could ride my route with me, help deliver 'em."

I say yes to that. Know I won't get nothing more out of it than a soft drink at the gas station, but I like going around in the Jeep, riding over back roads like Rippentuck and Cow House Run Road with

Dad. Can take a bag with me just in case, pick up any cans or bottles I happen to see.

That night Dad and I sit out on the porch. Ma's in the swing behind us shelling lima beans for next day, and Becky and Dara Lynn's in the grass catching lightning bugs and putting 'em in a jar. Dad laughs at the way Becky squeals when she gets a bug in her hand. But seeing those bugs in a jar reminds me of Shiloh all chained up at Judd's, a prisoner as sure as those bugs. Truth is, about everything reminds me of Shiloh. You once get a dog to look at you the way Shiloh looked at me, you don't forget it.

"Got seventeen!" Dara Lynn shouts. "Aren't they pretty, Ma?"

"Almost could turn off the electricity and let 'em light the kitchen," Ma says.

"You going to let 'em go?" I ask.

Dara Lynn shrugs.

"They'll die if you keep 'em in a jar," I tell her.

Becky, she comes over and crawls onto my lap. "We'll let 'em go, Marty," she says, and kisses me on the neck. A butterfly kiss, she calls it. Bats her eyelashes against me skin, feels like a moth's wings. She laughs and I laugh.

Then far off I hear a dog. Leastwise I think it's a dog. Might could be a fox cub, but I think, Shiloh.

"You hear that?" I ask Dad.

"Just a hound complaining," is all he says.

Next morning Dad gives me a nudge when he comes through to the kitchen, and I'm up like a shot. We ride to Sistersville and I haul all those catalogs out to the Jeep while Dad cases mail. Not everybody gets a catalog, of course, but anyone who places an order with Sears during the year get one, so there's lots to load up.

By quarter of nine, we're on the route; Dad pulls the Jeep up close to the mailboxes and I stuff the mail in, turn up the little red flag on the side, if there is one. Some folks even wait down at the box, and then you feel real bad if you don't have anything for them.

Dad knows everybody's name, though, and he always takes time to say a little somethin'.

" 'Mornin', Bill," he says to an old man whose face lights up like Christmas when we stop. "How's the wife doing?"

" 'Bout the same," the man says, "but this catalog sure going to cheer her." And he sets off for his house, mail tucked under his arm.

People even leave somethin' in their boxes once in awhile for Dad. Mrs. Ellison always leaves a little loaf of banana bread or a cinnamon roll, and Dad saves it to eat with his lunch.

After we finish Sistersville, we do the Friendly route, but as the Jeep gets up near Shiloh, my heart starts to pound. I'm thinking of closing my eyes tight in case the dog's around. If I see his eyes looking at me, they'll just drive me crazy. I can hear dogs barking when we're a half mile off from Judd Travers's trailer; dogs can pick up the sound of a Jeep that quick.

I get Judd's mail ready for him. He hasn't got any catalog coming, but he's got two other magazines that'll probably warm his heart— *Guns and Ammo* and *Shooting Times*. Why don't he take a magazine about dogs, I'm thinking—teach him how to be kind?

All the dogs is chained when we get to his place, so none's waiting for us at the box. But Judd is. He's got a big old sickle; is cutting weeds along his side of the road.

"'Mornin'," Dad says as the Jeep pulls up.

Judd straightens his back. His shirt's all soaked with sweat, and he wears this brown handkerchief tied around his forehead to keep the sweat from running in his eyes.

"How you doin', Ray?" he says, and comes over to the Jeep with his hand out. I give him his mail, and he even stinks like sweat. I know everybody sweats and everybody's sweat stinks, but seems to me Judd's sweat stinks worse than anyone's. Mean sweat.

"How come you aren't at work?" Dad says.

"You think this ain't work?" Judd answers, then laughs. "Got me a week of vacation coming, so I take a day now and then. This Friday I'm going hunting again. Take the dogs up on the ridge and see if I can get me some rabbit. Possum, maybe. Haven't had me a possum dinner for some time."

"Dogs okay?" Dad asks, and I know he's asking for me.

"Lean and mean," says Judd. "Keep 'em half starve, they'll hunt better."

"Got to keep 'em healthy, though, or you won't have 'em long," Dad says. I now he's saying that for me, too.

"Lose one, I'll buy another," Judd tells him.

I can't help myself. I lean out the window where I can see his face real good—big, round face, whiskers on his cheeks and chin where he hasn't shaved his face for five days—tight little eyes looking down on me beneath his bushy brows.

"That dog that followed me home the other day," I say. "He okay?"

"He's learnin'," Judd says. "Didn't give him a ounce of supper that night. Just put him where he could watch the others eat. Teach him not to wander off. Got him back in the shed, right now."

My stomach hurts for Shiloh. "That dog," I say again. "What's his name?"

Judd just laughs, and his teeth's dark where the tobacco juice oozes through. "Hasn't got a name. Never name any of my dogs. Dogs one, two, three, and four is all. When I want 'em, I whistle; when I don't, I give 'em a kick. 'Git,' 'Scram,' 'Out,' and 'Dammit'; *that's* my dogs' names." And he laughs, making the fat on his belly shake.

I'm so mad I can't see. I know I should shut my mouth, but it goes on talking. "His name's Shiloh," I say.

Judd looks down at me and spits sideways. Studies me a good long time, then shrugs as the Jeep moves forward again and on along the river.

Chapter 4

"Marty," Dad says when we're around the bend, "sometimes you haven't got the sense to shut up. You can't go tellin' a man what to call his dog."

But I'm mad, too. "Better than callin' him 'Git' or 'Scram.'"

"Judd Travers has the right to name his dog anything he likes or nothing at all. And you've got to get it through your head that it's *his* dog, not yours, and put your mind to other things."

The Jeep bounces along for a good long mile before I speak again. "I can't, Dad," I say finally.

And this time his voice is gentle: "Well, son, you got to try."

I eat my peanut-butter-and-soda-cracker sandwiches with Dad at noon, plus the zucchini bread Mrs. Ellsion had left in her mailbox for him, and after all the Sears catalogs and mail is delivered, we head back to the Sistersville post office. I get my Coca-Cola at the gas station while Dad finishes up, and we start home. I forget all about looking for cans and bottles. The can I'm holding is the only one I got.

"Judd Travers goes hunting near every weekend, don't he?" I ask Dad.

"I suppose he does."

"You can shoot at just about anything that moves?"

"Of course not. You can only shoot at what's in season."

I'm thinking how, 'bout a year ago, I was fooling around up on the ridge and come across a dead dog. A dead beagle, with a hole in its head. Never said anything because what was there to say? Somebody out hunting got a dog by mistake, I figured. It happens. But the more I think on it now, I wonder if it wasn't Judd Travers shooting a dog on purpose—shooting one of his own dogs that didn't please him.

Dad's still talking: "We've got a new game warden in the county, and I hear he's plenty tough. Used to be a man could kill a deer on his own property anytime if that deer was eating his garden; warden would look the other way. But they tell me the new warden will fine you good. Well, that's the way it ought to be, I guess."

"What if a man shoots a dog?" I ask.

Dad looks over at me. "Dogs aren't ever in season, Marty. Now you know that."

"But what if a man shoots one, anyway?"

"That would be up to the sheriff to decide what to do, I guess."

The next day I start early and set out on the main road to Friendly with a plastic bag. Get me eleven aluminum cans, but that's all. Could walk my legs off for a year and not even have enough to buy half a dog.

The questions I'd tried not think about before come back to me now. Would Judd Travers want to sell Shiloh at all? And how much would he want for him if he did? And even if I got Shiloh for my very own, how was I supposed to feed him?

There aren't many leftover scraps of anything in our house. Every extra bite of pork chop or boiled potato or spoonful of peas gets made into soup. If we'd had enough money for me to have dog and buy its food and pay the vet and everything, I would have had one by now. Dara Lynn's been begging for a cat for over a year. It isn't that we're rock-poor; trouble is that Grandma Preston's got real feeble, and she's being cared for by Dad's sister over in Clarksburg. Have to have nurses anytime Aunt Hettie goes out, and every spare cent we got goes to pay for Grandma's care. Nothing left over to feed dog. But I figure to get to that problem later on.

I wonder if maybe, in time, if I never see Shiloh again, I'll forget about him. But then I'm lying on the couch that night after everyone else has gone to bed, and I hear this far-off sound again, like a dog crying. Not barking, not howling, not whining even. Crying. And I get this awful ache in my chest. I wonder if it *is* a dog. If it's Shiloh.

"I know you want a dog, Marty," Ma says to me on Thursday. She's sitting at the kitchen table with cardboard boxes all around her, folding a stack of letters and putting them in envelopes. Ma gets work to do here at home anytime she can. "I wish we had the money so every one of you kids could have a pet. But with Grandma seeming to need more care, we just don't, and that's that."

I nod. Ma knows me better'n I know myself sometimes, but she don't have this straight. I don't want just any dog. I want Shiloh, because he needs me. Needs me bad.

It's Friday morning when I hear the sound. Dad's off on his mail route, Dara Lynn and Becky's watching cartoons on TV, Ma's out on the back porch washing clothes in the old washing machine that don't work—only the wringer part works if you turn it by hand. I'm sitting at the table eating a piece of bread spread with lard and jam when I hear the noise I know is Shiloh. Only the softest kind of noise—and right close.

I fold the bread up, jelly to the inside, stick it in my pocket, and go out the front door. Shiloh's under the sycamore, head on his paws, just like the day he followed me home in the rain. Soon as I see him, I know two things: (1) Judd Travers had taken his dogs out hunting, like he said, and Shiloh's run away from the pack, and (2) I'm not going to take him back. Not now, not ever.

I don't have time to think how I had promised Judd if I ever saw Shiloh loose again, I'd bring him back. Don't even think what I'm going to tell Dad. All I know right then is that I have to get Shiloh away from the house, where none of the family will see him. I run barefoot down the front steps and over to where Shiloh's lying, his tail just thumping like crazy in the grass.

"Shiloh!" I whisper, and gather him up in my arms. His body is shaking all over, but he don't try to get away, don't creep off from me the way he did that first day. I hold him as close and careful as I carry Becky when she's asleep, and I start off up the far hill into the woods, carrying my dog. I know that if I was to see Judd Travers that very minute with his rifle, I'd tell him he'd have to shoot me before I'd ever let him near Shiloh again.

There are burrs and stickers on the path up the hill, and usually I wouldn't take it without sneakers, but if there's burrs and stickers in my feet, I hardly feel 'em. Know Judd Travers and his hounds won't be over here, 'cause this hill belongs to my dad. Get me as far as the shadbush next to the pine, and then I sit down and hug Shiloh.

First time I really have him to myself—first time I can hug him, nobody looking, just squeeze his thin body, pat his head, stroke his ears.

"Shiloh," I tell him, as though he knows it's his name, "Judd Travers isn't never going to kick you again."

And the way his eyes look at me then, the way he reaches up and licks my face, it's like it seals the promise. I'd made a promise to Judd Travers I wasn't going to keep, Jesus help me. But I'm making one to Shiloh that I *will*, God strike me dead.

I set him down at last and go over to the creek for a drink of water. Shiloh follows along beside me. I cup my hands and drink, and Shiloh helps himself, lapping it up. Now what? I ask myself. The problem is looking me square in the face.

I got to keep Shiloh a secret. That much I know. But I'm not going to keep him chained. Only thing I can think of is to make him a pen. Don't like the idea of it, but I'll be with him as much as I can.

I take him back to the shadbush and Shiloh lays down.

"Shiloh," I say, patting his head. "Stay!"

He thumps his tail. I start to walk away, looking back. Shiloh gets up. "Stay!" I say again, louder, and point to the ground.

He lays back down, but I know he's like to follow, anyways. So I pull him over to a pine tree, take the belt off my jeans, loop it through the raggedy old collar Shiloh's wearing, and fasten the belt to the tree. Shiloh don't like it much, but he's quiet. I go down the path and every so often I turn around. Shiloh is looking at me like he won't never see me again, but he don't bark. Strangest thing I've ever seen in a dog, to be that still.

Ma's still on the back porch. When she washes, it takes her near all day. Dara Lynn and Becky's stuck to the TV. So I go to the shed by the side of the house and I take the extra fencing Dad used when we had us more chickens. I take me a piece of wire, too, and go back up the hill.

Shiloh's still there, and he don't try to get up while I set to work. I string the fencing around the trunks of three small trees, for corner posts, and then back to the pine tree again where I fasten it with wire. Pen measures about six by eight feet.

I go back down to the shed again, and this time I get the old rotten planks Dad took out of the back steps when he put in the new. Pick me up an old pie tin, too. I take the planks up to Shiloh's pen and make him a lean-to at one end, to protect him from rain. Fill the pie tin with water so's he'll have something to drink.

Last of all, I take the lard bread from my pocket and feed it to Shiloh in little pieces, letting him lick my fingers after every bite. I wrap my arms around him, pat him, run my hands over his ears, even kiss his nose. I tell him about a million times I love him as much as I love my ma.

The worry part is whether or not he'll stay quiet. I'm hoping he will, 'cause he was a silent dog to begin with, but all the way back down the hill to the house, I put my finger to my lips and turn back.

"Shhh!" I say.

Shiloh, he don't make a sound. Like he had the bark beat out of him when he was a pup and it just never come back.

I'm tense as a cricket that night. Tense when Dad drives up in his Jeep, afraid the dog will bark. Tense when Dara Lynn and Becky are out in the yard playing after dinner, squealin' and yellin', afraid that Shiloh will want to get in on the fun and maybe dig a hole under the fence. He never comes.

I manage to take a piece of potato and some cornbread up to him before it gets dark. I sit down in his pen with him, and he crawls all over me, licking my face. If he'd been a cat, he would have purred, he was that glad to see me.

Tell him I'm coming back tomorrow with some kind of leash for him. Tell him we're going to run all over that hill, him and me, every day. Tell him he's my dog now, and I'm not never going to let anybody hurt him again ever, and then I leave, wiring that fence good. I go home and sleep a full night, first time in a long while.

Chapter 5

I GOT TO TAKE one problem at a time, I tell myself.

Problem number one: where to keep Shiloh hid. Solved.

Problem number two: Would Shiloh be quiet? Yes, he would.

Problem number three: How am I going to get food out of the house, enough to feed Shiloh twice a day, without Ma noticing?

The next morning before breakfast, as soon as Dad's gone, I take a biscuit from the kitchen and a rope from the shed outside, and run up the far hill before Ma and Dara Lynn and Becky get out of bed.

This time Shiloh's on his feet waiting for me, tail going like a windshield wiper, fast speed. A soft yip of pure joy cuts off quick when I say "Shhh!" but as soon as I'm in the pen, Shiloh's leaping up almost shoulder high to lick my cheek, nuzzling my hands, my thighs. He gulps down the biscuit I give him. Wants more, I can tell, but he don't bark. Seems to know he's safe only as long as he's quiet. I tie the rope to his collar.

"Shiloh, boy we're goin' for a run," I tell him.

To get in and out of Shiloh's pen, I got to unfasten the piece of wire that holds the fencing against the trunk of the pine, then move the fencing aside long enough to slip out. Shiloh lets me go through first, he follows, and then we're both together, like a six-legged animal, pounding along up the path, legs bumping, Shiloh leaping up to lick my hand. I let go of the rope and let Shiloh run free for awhile. If he goes ahead even a few steps, he stops and looks back to see if I'm coming; if he stops to sniff at a tree or bush and I go on by, his feet pound double time to catch up.

Just out of the woods on the other side of the hill, there's a meadow, and I slump down it the grass to rest. Shiloh's all over me, licking my face sloppy wet. I giggle and roll over on my stomach, covering my head and neck with my arms. Shiloh whines and nudges his nose under my shoulder, working to roll me over. I laugh and turn on my back, pulling Shiloh down onto my chest, and for a while we both lay there, panting, enjoying the sunshine, belonging to each other.

"What'd you do today, Marty?" Dad asks as he gets out of his Jeep late that evening.

"Oh, looked for ground hogs up on the hill. Fooled around," I tell him.

"How's the can collecting coming?"

"Found some a couple days ago."

"Saw some bottles in the ditch down near Doe Murphy's," Dad says.

"I'll go take a look," I tell him and set out with my bag. I have to keep collecting cans, enough to cover some money for meat and bones from the grocer down in Friendly. The bigger Shiloh grows, the more he'll eat.

When I get back home, supper's on the table, and I slip into my chair just as Dad asks the blessing: "Dear Lord, we thank you for the food you've provided for our table. Bless it to nourish the good within us. Amen."

Ma picks up the meat loaf and passes it around, and the meal begins.

I eat about half my supper, then say, "I been getting this sort of full feeling at dinner, Ma, and then I'm hungry again before I go to bed." Ma don't even look up. "Well, don't eat so much at dinner, then, and eat again before bedtime."

"Food'll be all gone by then."

"There's always cornflakes or something."

"But I get hungry for meat and potatoes later."

"Save some back, then."

"Dara Lynn'll eat it."

"For goodness' sake, Marty!" says Ma.

"Who wants cold meat loaf?" Dara Lynn says.

Forks continue clinking on the table; Becky keeps digging her fork in her boiled potato. No one looks up. No one pauses. No one even questions. Easy as falling off a log.

I get up from the table finally and put some of my meat loaf and half a potato on a saucer.

"I'm puttin' this in the fridge, Dara Lynn," I say. "Don't you go pickin' at it."

"I *won't*, I told you!" she says.

I go into the other room and sit down on the sofa. So far, so good.

"You seem restless, Marty," Ma calls.

"Me? Heck, no. I got lots to do."

"Where's David Howard this summer? Haven't seen him around."

"Think he went to Tennessee to visit his uncle."

"Fred? Michael?"

"Haven't seen Fred. Michael's gone to some kind of camp."

"You're not lonely?"

"How and I be lonely with the whole outdoors to play in?" I answer. Wish they'd get off my back.

"You can ride along to work with me again anytime you want," says Dad.

I pick up the comic book I bought a few weeks back. "I want to go, I'll let you know," I tell him.

Gradually the kitchen clatter dies down. Dad belches and goes out on the back porch to look at the sky, same as he always does. Becky's fooling with her food, and ma sends her away from the table. Dara Lynn giggles at Becky and gets asked to clear the dishes.

I wait until everyone is out of the kitchen and sitting around on the back porch to catch the breeze. As usual Becky and Dara Lynn whoop and tumble around in the grass., glad for an audience, and after I sit a respectable amount of time, I say, "Think I'll take my .22 and go up the far hill awhile."

"What you figure on shooting this time of evening?" Dad asks.

"Just workin' on my aim," I tell him. "See how good I can hit when the light's dim."

"Don't you ever, never, aim your gun toward this house or yard," Ma says.

"I'll point it dead away," I promise. I go back inside for my gun, slip the leftover food from the saucer into a little plastic sack, and set off up the hill, the sounds of my sisters' shouts and giggles behind me.

Again, as I get near the pen, I hear soft, happy yips. But soon as I say, "Shhh!" the noise stops. The only sound you can hear is the swishing of Shiloh's tail, hitting the fence, the soft pad of his paws as he leaps up in the air in sheer, pure happiness; the sloppy slap of his jowls together as he gobbles down the supper I've brought him and then he commences to slobber love all over me as well.

I unhook the wire, push the fence open, and lead Shiloh to the stream for a drink, filling the pie pan with fresh water. When I lead him back to the pen again, I can tell he's disappointed, wanted to go for a run, but I give him enough hugging and squeezing and petting to last the night, with the promise of another run through the meadow the next day.

I'm halfway down the hill when I remember I haven't fired my gun once, and wonder if Dad will say anything. By the time I reach the back porch though, the whole family's facing down the driveway, 'cause there's the sound of a truck motor growing louder and louder.

I stop in my tracks, fingers tightening around my gun.

Dad, sitting on the edge of the porch, leans forward so he can see. "Looks like Judd Travers's pickup," he says.

My chest feels tight, like I'm having trouble breathing.

The truck pulls up by the side of the house, and the door swings open.

"Evenin'!" Dad calls out as Judd, wearing his old western-style boots with the sharp heel, gets out and comes over.

"Evenin'," he says.

"You had dinner?" Ma asks. "I got some leftovers I could heat up real quick."

"Had me some ribs already," he says. "Ain't looking for a meal, Mrs. Preston, I'm looking for a dog." He sure don't waste any time getting to the point. Now my heart's really pounding.

"That new dog of yours run off again?" Dad asks him.

"I swear to God I find him this time, I'm goin' to break his legs," Judd says, and spits.

"Oh, come on, Judd. A dog with four broke legs ain't no dog to you at all."

"He's no dog to me at a all the way he keeps runnin' off. It's the fourth time he's left the pack when I had him out huntin'. I got to teach him a lesson. Whup him good and starve him lean. Wondered if you'd seen him."

"I sure didn't see him on my route today, and you know if I had, I'd have put him in the Jeep and brought him to you straight away," says Dad.

"What about that boy of yours? Think he's seen him?"

Dad had heard me coming back from the hill, and he turns around. "Marty?"

I stand rooted to the ground at the side of the house. "What?"

"Come on around here. Judd's dog's missing again and he wants to know have you seen him."

"H-his dog? Here in the yard? Haven't seen any dog of any kind in our yard all day," I say, coming a few steps closer.

Judd is sure studying me hard. So is Dad.

"Well, how about when you went out looking for bottles?" Dad asks. "You see him then?"

"Nope." My voice is stronger now. "Saw that big German shepherd of Baker's that gets loose sometimes, and saw a little old gray dog, but sure didn't see that beagle."

"Well, you keep an eye out sharp," Judd says, "and if you see him, you throw a rope around him, drag him over. Hear?"

I only look at him. Can't speak. Can't even nod my head. I wouldn't never promise him that.

"You hear what he asked you, Marty?" says Dad.

I nod my head, Yes, I heard, all right.

"Okay, then," Judd says, and gets back in his pickup.

"Have any luck hunting yesterday?" Dad calls after him.

"A rabbit. Saw a groundhog but didn't get it. That new dog hadn't run off, he would've got it for me. He wasn't such a good hunting dog, I would have shot him by now."

"Sheriff would get on you if you do somethin' like that, Judd."

"Law never told me before what I could do with my dogs, won't be tellin' me now," Judd says. He laughs, waves his hand, starts the engine, and the pickup pulls away.

Chapter 6

Night in West Virginia is as dark as black can be. No car lights sweepin' across my walls or ceiling like when I stay overnight with David Howard down in Friendly. No street lamps shinin' in the windows, no lights from next-door houses. Where I live, there ain't no street lamps at all, no house close enough to see from our windows.

My eyes are open, anyway. I stare up into the darkness of the living room and the darkness stares back.

I'm remembering how once, several years ago, when Ma bought milk chocolate rabbits one Easter for me and Dara Lynn, I'd finished eating mine, but Dara Lynn took only a nibble of hers every day or so, keeping it up on her dresser in its pink and yellow tinfoil, driving me nuts. And one day I just crept in there and ate off one of that rabbit's ears. Dara Lynn, of course, threw a fit, and when Ma asked me if I'd done it, I said no. I could feel my cheeks and neck burning red.

"You *sure*, Marty?" she asked. I'd only nodded and left the room. It was one of the worst days of my life.

About an hour later she come out on the porch where I was pushing myself slow in the swing and sat down beside me.

"You know, Marty," she said, "Dara Lynn don't know who ate the ear off her candy rabbit and I don't know who did it, but Jesus knows. And right this very minute Jesus is looking down with the saddest eyes on the person who ate that chocolate. The Bible says that the worst thing that can ever possibly happen to us is to be separated forever from God's love. I hope you'll keep that in mind."

I just swallowed and didn't say anything. But before I went to bed, when Ma asked me again about that rabbit, I gulped and said yes, and she made me get down on my knees and ask God's forgiveness, which wasn't so bad. I honestly felt better afterward. But then she said that Jesus wanted me to go in the next room and tell Dara Lynn what I'd done, and Dara Lynn had a fit all over again. Threw a box of Crayolas at me and could have broke my nose. Called me a rotten, greedy pig. If *that* made Jesus sad, Ma never said.

Now as I study the darkness in the room around me, I'm thinking about lies again. I *hadn't* lied to Judd Travers when I said I hadn't seen his dog in the yard today. That was the honest-to-God truth, because Shiloh hadn't been anywhere near our yard. But I also know that you can lie not only by what you say but what you don't say. Nothing I'd told Judd was an outright lie, but what I'd kept inside myself made him think that I hadn't seen his dog at all.

"Jesus," I whisper finally, "which you want me to do? Be one hundred percent honest and carry that dog back to Judd so that one of your creatures can be kicked and starved all over again, or keep him here and fatten him up to glorify your creation?"

The question seemed to answer itself, and I'm pretty proud of that prayer. Repeat it to myself so's to remember it in case I need to use it again. If Jesus is anything like the story cards from Sunday school make him out to be, he ain't the kind to want a thin, little beagle to be hurt.

The problem's more mixed-up than that, though. I'm lying to my folks as well. I'm *not* eating the leftover meat loaf I've put away. Every bit of food saved is money saved that could go to buy Dara Lynn a new pair of sneakers so Ma won't have to cut open the tops of her old ones to give her toes more room. Every little bit of food wasted is money wasted. If we ever have the least little bit of money to spare that doesn't have to go for the care of Grandma Preston, first thing we all want is a telephone so we don't have to ride down to Doc Murphy's to use his. But the way I figure, if it's food from my own plate I would have eaten myself but don't, what's the harm in that?

Next morning when I get up to see Shiloh, I put the rope on his collar and lead him to the other side of the hill again, out of sight of all but God. Then I let him go, and we race and tumble and laugh and roll, stopping now and then just to lie in the clover, me on my back, Shiloh on his stomach, both of us panting and nuzzling each other.

Don't know if Shiloh's gettin' more human or I'm gettin' to be more dog. If Jesus ever comes back to earth again, I'm thinking, he'll come as a dog, because there isn't anything as humble or patient or loving or loyal as the dog I have in my arms right now.

We eat our Sunday meal, but by late afternoon, storm clouds roll in, and the rain beats down on the tin roof of our house, streaming down the window glass, making a small pond in the side yard.

I can't help staring out the window at the far hill. Will Shiloh—*can* he, even—leap that fence to try and go somewhere it's more dry?

Is he smart enough to go under that lean-to I'd made for him? Have I built it right, away from the wind? What if he gets to howling?

In twenty minutes the rain stops, though, the sun comes out, the birds start to sing again—all those worms oozing up through the wet mud. Shiloh's stayed where he was, trusting me that where I put him was best. Being quiet, like he know his life depends on it.

"Marty," Dad says, going outside with a rag to wipe off his Jeep. "I saw Mrs. Howard yesterday and she said David was back from Tennessee, wanting to know when you boys could get together. She said David would like to come up here someday next week."

I like David Howard fine, but I sure don't want him up here. David likes the hill; always wants to play there. He's not afraid of snakes the way Dara Lynn is. David, in fact, likes to go to the very top of that hill and then go running lickety-split down it, racing to see who's first to the fence at the bottom. Likes to climb the trees up there, too, and play lookout.

"Well, I'll go down to David's tomorrow," I say. "I'd rather do that."

"Why not do both?" Ma says, coming out to throw some mash to the hens. "You've hardly seen any friends all summer, Marty. Why don't you go down to Friendly one afternoon and ask David to come up here another?"

"There's nothing much to do up here," I say, not knowing how else to answer.

It was the wrong answer. Both Ma and Dad were looking at me now.

"You said just the other day you had plenty to do here," Dad tells me, wringing out his rag at the pump.

"Lots for me to do, but not much for David Howard," I say. *A lie.* That's a flat-out lie. Funny how one lie leads to another and before you know it, your whole life can be a lie.

I sit on the porch swing later, not even bothering to push it, and listen to the table being set inside.

"What you figure is wrong with that boy, Lou?" Dad's voice.

"Just being eleven, I guess," Ma tells him. "Eleven's a moody age. Was for me, anyways."

"You think that's all it is?"

"What pleases you one day don't please you at all the next. What more do *you* think it is?"

"Don't think he's got that dog on his mind still, do you?"

"Eleven's got about everything on its mind," Ma answers.

And then the evening news comes on, and Dara Lynn and Becky come out to the porch, leaving the TV to Daddy.

Dara Lynn's got the devil in her tonight—little bit bored with summer, but not quite ready for school to start. Just for devilment, she plunks herself down beside me in that swing and starts doin' everything I do. I sigh, she sighs. I rest my arms on my head, she does the same. Gits Becky doin' it, too, both of 'em laughin' to beat the band.

When I have my fill of this nonsense, I decide to go up the hill and see how Shiloh's doin', but as I go down off the porch, Dara Lynn gits up and makes as if to follow me.

I stop. "I'm lookin' to find me a snake stick," I say as if to myself.

"I'm lookin' to find me a snake stick," Dara Lynn says.

I don't pay her no mind at all. Just start walkin' along the edge of the yard, picking up a stick here, a stick there, Dara Lynn tagging along behind.

"It's go the have the longest handle and a good strong fork on the end," I say, "because that was the biggest, meanest snake I ever saw in my life."

Dara Lynn stops dead still. She couldn't say all that right if she tried, but she's not interested anymore in trying. "*What* snake?" she says.

"Snake I saw up on the hill this mornin'," I tell her. "Must have been four, five feet long, just lookin' for somebody's leg to wrap itself around."

Dara Lynn don't go a step farther. Becky don't even come down off the porch.

"What you going to do when you find it?" Dar Lynn asks.

"Try to keep it from bitin' me, first. Pick it up with my stick, second, put it in a sack, and carry it clear on up past the Shiloh school-house, let it out in the woods there. Won't kill it unless I have to."

"Kill it!" says Dara Lynn. "Git you gun and blow its head off."

"You been watchin' too much stuff on TV, Dara Lynn," I tell her. "Even snakes got the right to live." I'm thinking how if I ever become a vet's helper, I got to take care of pet snakes, too.

Next day, to head off David Howard from riding up from Friendly on his bike, I go down to see him. I'd tended to Shiloh first, taking a fistful of scrambled eggs left over from breakfast, a bit of bacon, and a half slice of whole wheat toast that I stuck in my jeans pocket. It's not enough for the dog, I know, but probably more than he'd get from Judd.

It's not enough for me, either. Sneaking off half my breakfast, lunch, and dinner for Shiloh like I'm doing means me going half hungry all the time, but if I eat extra, then it means Shiloh's costing us money we can't afford. I fill my pockets with wormy peaches before I set out for Friendly, biting off each piece, spitting it out in my hand, and picking out the worms before I put it back in my mouth.

It pleased me that Shiloh was sleepin' in his lean-to when I'd gone up that morning. The ground was dry under there, and I'd brought up some old gunnysacks from the shed for him to lie on, made it seem more like a bed to him, more like a home.

The walk to Friendly take a good long time unless I hitch a ride. I'm not allowed to get in a car with somebody I don't know, but Dad being the mail carrier for this part of the county, I know most everybody who goes by. The first person to come along this morning, though, is Judd Travers.

When I hear the sound of a motor and turn to see his truck slowin' down, I turn forward again and keep on walkin', but he pulls up beside me.

"Want a lift?" he sings out.

"No, thanks," I say "Almost there."

"Where you goin'?"

I couldn't think fast enough to lie. "David Howard's."

"Hell, boy, you ain't even halfway. Hop in."

I know I don't have to unless I want, but if he's already suspicious about me, that'll only make it worse. So I get in.

"See my dog yet?" First thing out of his mouth.

"I been lookin' over all the roads," I tell him in answer. "No beagle."

"Well, I don't think he'd stick to roads," Judd says. "Not a dog as shy as him. Shy as a field mouse, 'cept when he's around rabbits. That's what the man said who sold him to me, and he sure was right about that."

"How much did you pay for him?" I ask.

"Got him cheap 'cause he's shy. Thirty-five dollars. Worth a lot more'n that as a hunting dog, if I could just keep that damned animal home."

"You got to treat a dog good if you want him to stick around," I say, bold as brass.

"What you know about it?" Judd jerks his head in my direction, then turns the other way and spits his tobacco out the window. "You never even had a dog, did you?"

"I figure a dog's the same as a kid. You don't treat a kid right, he'll run off first chance he gets, too."

Judd laughs. "Well, if that was true, I would have run away when I was four. Far back as I can remember, Pa took the belt to me—big old welts on my back so raw I could hardly pull my shirt on. I stuck around. Didn't have anyplace else to go. I turned out, didn't I?"

"Turned out how?" The boldness in my chest is growing, taking up all the air.

Now Judd sounds mad. "You tryin' to be smart with me, boy?"

"No. Just asking how you turned out, somebody who was beat since he was four. I feel sorry, is what I feel."

Judd's real quiet a moment. The big old wad of tobacco in his cheek bobs up and down. "Well, don't go wasting your sorry on me," he says. "Nobody ever felt sorry for me, and I never felt sorry for nobody else. Sorry's something I can do without."

I don't say anything at all.

We reach the road where David Howard lives, and the truck slows down.

"I can walk from here," I tell him. "Thanks." I get out.

But as I come around the truck to cross the street, Judd leans out the window. "Like I said, that dog's a shy one. Don't think you'll see much of him near the road, but you keep your eye out for him the in the fields. That's where he'll be, more'n likely. You see him, all you got to do is whistle. That's what I teach him. I whistle and he comes to me, he gits fed. But he does somethin' I don't like, I kick him clear to China. You see him, just whistle, then hang on to him and I'll come pick him up. You hear?"

"I hear," I tell him, and keep walking.

Chapter 7

DAVID HOWARD'S HOUSE is about twice as big as ours for about half as many people. Only him and his ma and dad. Mr. Howard works for the *Tyler Star-News* in Sistersville, and David's ma is a teacher. They're always glad to have me come down to visit, partly because David and I are best friends, and partly, I think, because their old house is so big, the three of 'em get lost in it.

It's got two floors—three counting the basement and four counting the attic. Has four bedrooms upstairs: one for David, one for his folks, one just for company, and one for his father's books, with a computer in it. Downstairs there's a big kitchen, a dining room with a fancy light hanging over the table, a parlor, and a side room with lots of windows just for plants, plus a porch that runs along three sides of the house. I told Ma once the Howards had a room just for company, a room just for books, and a room just for plants, and she said that was three rooms too many. First time I ever saw any envy in my ma.

David says the house used to belong to his great-granddaddy, so I figure it'll get to be David's someday. Like maybe our little house and the hill and meadow and the far woods will belong to me and Shiloh, except I'd probably have to share it with Dara Lynn and Becky and whoever they marry, and that's a whole lot of people for four rooms.

"Marty!" Mrs. Howard says when I ring their doorbell that sounds like church chimes. "We're *so* glad to see you! Come on in!"

She always means it, too. It's as though she thinks about me even when I'm not there. Then David comes whooping downstairs, carrying the helicopter that flies when you pull a string, and pretty soon we're out in the backyard, chasing around after the helicopter and telling each other what we've been doing the six weeks since school let out. I got to bite my tongue not to let on about Shiloh.

We sit on David's back steps and eat Popsicles his ma makes out of pineapple juice. I tell David about the fox I saw with a gray body and a red head, and he tells me about is aunt's Siamese cat that yowls just for the pure joy of making noise. Then I tell him about Judd Travers and how mean he is to his dogs, not mentioning Shiloh, of course, and then David says he's got this surprise to show me.

We go upstairs to his room and David says he got a pet and asks do I want to hold it.

"Sure!" I tell him. "What is is?"

"Sit down and close your eyes and hold out your hands," says David.

I sit down on the edge of his bed and close my eyes and hold out my hands. I expect something warm and wiggly and furry to plop into my arms. Instead I feel something cold and round and plastic, and when I look, it's a fishbowl with sand in it and a hermit crab, scurrying around with a shell on its back. This is a *pet*?

"My first pet!" David says. "His name is Hermie. See all those shells in there? We bought them for him. At night he gets out of one and puts on another, just like changing clothes."

I look at David and I look at that crab in a fishbowl and I want to tell him about Shiloh and how we run up and down the far side of the hill every day and roll in the grass and how he licks my face, but I can't tell him anything. Not yet. Not ever, maybe.

Hermie's sort of fun, though. We get out David's old blocks—the kind you play with back in kindergarten—and we build this big maze with walls on both sides, and then we put Hermie in it. He skids along the maze, looking which way to go, and we laugh when he gets himself in a dead end. I guess any kind of pet's okay once you get used to it, but I wouldn't trade Shiloh for all the hermit crabs in the world.

"When can I come up to your house?" David asks me when we put the blocks away.

"I don't know," I tell him. "Ma's had this sort of headache lately, and she can't take any noise at all." Boy, I am sure asking for trouble with that one.

"We could stay out on that big hill," David suggests. "Chase around in that field. Play lookout."

"Don't think we ought to till she's feeling better," I say. "I'll let you know. But I can come down here again next week, maybe."

I tell Mrs. Howard I got to be home by late afternoon to help out, and she say surely I can stay for lunch, which is what I was hoping. I sit down at the table with place mats, which are little doll-size tablecloths, one under each plate. Mrs. Howard's made us each a chicken-salad sandwich with lettuce and tomato, and toothpicks with olives on top to hold it all together. David's ma is like that. I think it's because she's a teacher—always looking for ways to make something better than it is.

She does the same with boys. She don't just leave us to eat by ourselves. My ma packs us a lunch and lets us eat it out in the woods. Mrs. Howard always sits down to eat with us and talks about grown-up things. Today she tells us about how we've got some new people elected to office who are going to be more honest, she hopes, than the people they defeated, and how the county's going to be better because of it, and so will the whole state of West Virginia. David's ma thinks big.

"You can't just go on electing people to government because they were friends of your father or grandfather," she says, chewing on a bite of celery.

Mostly I'm thinking about the food. I eat every bit of my chicken sandwich. I'm so hungry I don't even save some for Shiloh; then I'm ashamed of myself. Mrs. Howard notices the way I pick up every little crumb, and she says, "I've got enough chicken salad left for another half a sandwich, Marty. Would you like it?"

"Sure would taste good on the walk back home," I tell her, and she sets right to work wrapping it up for me. *Shiloh's dinner*, I tell myself.

But lunch isn't over yet. After the sandwich there's tapioca pudding and chocolate-covered graham crackers, which I love almost as much as Christmas. I don't see any way to get the pudding to Shiloh, so I eat that, but I ask can I take a couple cookies along to eat on the way home, too, and she opens the sack and sticks in six cookies. Ma would have blushed with shame if she heard me ask this, but seems I'm at the point where I'll do most anything for Shiloh. A lie don't seem a lie anymore when it's meant to save a dog, and right and wrong's all mixed up in my head.

Worse than that, when I leave David's home, I don't even head home. First I go down the street to the corner store and ask Mr. Wallace does he have any sort of old cheese or lunch meat he can sell me cheap. I got fifty-three cents for the cans I collected so far that Dad turned in for me, and I show Mr. Wallace how much I got.

"Well, Marty, let me see what I can find back here," he says, leading me into the little room behind the counter. He's sort of talking without looking at me, the way folks do when they don't want to embarrass you. "I got some stuff here that's not exactly spoiled, but it's too old to sell. Wouldn't want your family getting sick on it, though."

I blush then, 'cause my dad would die of embarrassment if he knew what Mr. Wallace is thinking—that I'm buying this food for our supper, but there's no way in the world I can let on about Shiloh.

I give him all the change I got, and he lets me have a big hunk of cheese, moldy on one side, a carton of sour cream, and half a package of frankfurters that somebody opened and bought five of. I'm happy as a flea on a dog. Somehow I know without asking that Mr. Wallace isn't going to go tellin' folks about it, because people around here tend to keep quiet out of someone else's business.

Next problem I got to solve, though, is how to keep all this stuff from spoiling in the July heat. Can't keep it in our refrigerator or Ma would notice right off. When I get home, Ma's ironing and watching TV and Dara Lynn and Becky's out on the front swing with paper dolls spread out all over the place, so I fish around out in the shed till I find me an old Hi-C can.

I sneak off up the hill with the can and all the food I got with me. Then, with Shiloh watching, I put a rock in the bottom of the can to hold it down, set it in the cool stream, surround it with rocks, and put the container of sour cream, the frankfurters, and the cheese and cookies in there. Put the plastic lid on and set a large rock on top to keep the raccoons out. I'm so proud of myself I like to crow. Hungry again, too, but that half chicken-salad sandwich from Mrs. Howard is Shiloh's dinner, and I give it to him right off.

After that Shiloh and me go on a good long run over the meadow on the far side of the hill, and after I take him back, put fresh water in the pie pan, and love him good, I start down the hill. Halfway to the bottom, here comes Dara Lynn.

"What *you* doin' up here?" I ask her, heart starting to thump.

"Just wanted to see what *you're* doing," she complains. "You go up here every day almost."

"You leave Becky by herself while Ma's ironing?"

"Becky's okay." She turns and follows me back down the hill. Shiloh, up in the pen, don't make a sound. That's how smart a dog he is.

"Well, I was lookin' for that snake again, but he's hiding from me good," I tell her.

"You *still* didn't get him?" she asks, and when I look back, she's got her eyes to the left, then to the right. "You didn't even take your snake stick," she says. *She's* a smart one, too.

"Got me a stick back up on the hill," I tell her.

"How many snakes you figure are up there, Marty?"

"Oh . . . 'bout twenty-nine that you can see. Baby snakes all over the place, though, hiding. Growing into big ones all the time."

Dara Lynn's walking faster now, hurrying to git on by me, watching every place she sets her foot.

I don't feel good about the lies I tell Dara Lynn or David or his ma. But don't feel exactly bad, neither. If what Grandma Preston told me once about heaven and hell is true, and liars go to hell, then I guess that's where I'm headed. But she also told me that only people are allowed in heaven, not animals. And if I was to go to heaven and look down to see Shiloh left below, head on his paws, I'd run away from heaven sure.

Chapter 8

NEXT TWO DAYS go by smooth as buttermilk. Shiloh gets biscuits or toast and a couple bites of ham for breakfast, and then in the evening, I fix him up some frankfurters, cut up and mixed with sour cream, and little chunks of cheese. He don't much like the cheese. It sticks to his teeth and he turns his head sideways when he chews, trying to get it off. Licks his chops afterward, though.

He throws up the first time he eats the stuff—too rich for his belly, I guess—but after that he manages to keep it down, and all the while he's fattening out a little. Each day it's harder to see his ribs.

I know my secret can't go on forever, though. Only had the dog for six days, and that evening I find out that Judd Travers wants to hunt on our land. Up the hill and over in the far woods. Thinks maybe he could find himself some quail over there, he says.

When Dad tells us that piece of news at dinner, my whole body goes cold. I want to jump up and scream, "No!" but I just grip my chair and wait it out.

"Ray, I don't like that idea at all," Ma says. "You never ask to hunt on his land, and I don't want him hunting on ours. If we let him, we've got to let anyone else who asks, and one of those shots could find its way down here."

"I'll tell him no," Dad says. "Don't like the idea of it myself. I'll tell him the kids play up there."

I stopped gripping my chair, but my heart still goes on thumping hard. I'm thinking how maybe Judd Travers has hold of the idea that I got his dog hid up there and he's looking for an excuse to snoop around. Having Shiloh a secret is like a bomb waiting to go off.

Next day Dad comes home with more news—good news to him, bad news to me.

"Can't figure it out," he says, walkin' through the door with a sack in his hands. "Folks are taking to leavin' me food in their mailboxes, Lou. Used to be it was just Mrs. Ellison and her banana bread, but found me a ham sandwich today in Nora Klingle's box and half a baked pie in the Saunders'. I look thin to you or something?"

Ma laughs. "Maybe it's just you're the best mail carrier they ever had on the route."

"Well, we got half a pie for dessert tonight, anyways," Dad says.

Oh, brother! I say to myself. Maybe Mr. Wallace is doing more talking than I figured. He wouldn't come right out and tell folks I was in his store buying cheap food, but he might just pass it along that the Preston family's in hard times, and suddenly food starts appearing. That's the way it is here.

The next day, Ma rides into town with Dad, taking the girls along, and goes s shopping for new sneakers for Dara Lynn and socks and underpants for Becky. First time I have the whole place to myself, and I let Shiloh run pure free. Bring him down the hill to the house, feed him the heels off a loaf of new bread, all the leftover sausage from breakfast, and a bowl of milk. Then I let him lick the oatmeal pan.

Show him every one of our four rooms, hold him in my lap on the porch swing, and laugh when he tries to stand up on the seat himself while the swing's moving. I let him smell the couch where I sleep and crawl under the front steps to sniff out the mole lives under there, follow him all over creation when he takes out after a rabbit. Then he gives up when he sees I'm not going to shoot that rabbit no way.

But I figure my luck's going to run out if I don't get him back to his pen soon, so about noon I take him back, and he goes right to the gunnysacks in the lean-to, he's so tuckered out.

It's just in time, 'cause when I get back and get the dishes done for Ma, the house picked up some, I look out and here she comes up the lane with Dara Lynn and Becky and their packages. Somebody gave 'em a lift; you can always count on that around Friendly.

Ma's pleased I got the dishes done, I can tell.

"Nice to come back to a clean house, Marty," she tells me. "Had some luck with my shopping, too. Wasn't a thing I bought that wasn't on sale."

Dara Lynn's wore her new sneakers home and got a blister already, but she don't care, she's so glad to have something new.

When I walk in the kitchen next, Ma's looking at her face in the mirror over the sink. Got her eyebrows raised high, then she pushes them low, then raises them again. When she sees me studying her, she says, "Marty, I got frown lines on my face? Tell me the truth now."

I look at her good. "Sure don't see any," I say. I don't neither. Ma's got a pretty face. Plain, but smooth.

"Well, I don't, either, but two people this morning asked me how I was feeling and one of 'em wants to tell me what to take for headaches. I figure that if folks think I have headaches, I must be doing a lot of frowning."

Whomp, whomp, whomp. That's my heart. "Folks think they got a remedy for something, they'll tell it to you whether you need it or not," I say. Sound so grown-up I hardly recognize myself. So scared inside, though, my stomach's shaking.

Ma's taking out all the things she's bought and putting 'em on the table, taking the price tags off Becky's underpants and socks. "I saw David's mother at the dollar store," she says, "and they've got relatives coming in tonight. She wanted to know if she could bring David up here tomorrow when the rest of them go to Parkersburg. I told her yes."

"Okay," I say, but all the while I'm thinking what I'm going to do with David to keep him off that hill. Take him up toward the old Shiloh schoolhouse, maybe, and walk along the river. Funny thing is, you've got yourself a dog, you sometimes feel like you don't need anyone else. Used to be I'd be waiting at the window for David Howard to come up here for a visit. Nobody else loves you as much as a dog. Except your ma, maybe.

That night Ma makes us fried chicken for supper. First time in along while. I put away a wing and a thigh on a saucer—to eat later, I tell Ma—and add a spoonful of squash, which might be good for Shiloh's insides. He eats anything. The frankfurters and cheese and sour cream is all gone, so I got to be watching for table scraps again and go out can collecting soon.

Dad's working on the pickup after dinner—changing the oil— Becky and Dara Lynn's turning somersaults in the grass, and Ma's cleaning the kitchen. Soon as her back is turned, I sneak the food off the saucer and head up the hill to see Shiloh.

I can tell Shiloh likes the fried chicken better than he liked the sour cream-frankfurter mess he'd been eating all week. Even eats the squash, and then he licks my hands and fingers to get all the salt off, anyplace I'd touched a piece of chicken.

Since I'd already taken him all over creation that morning, I don't feel he'll miss much if I don't take him out again, so I go around scooping up all the dog doo, like I do every day, toss it over the fence, and then I lie down on my back in the grass and cover my face with my arms, our favorite game. Shiloh goes nuts trying to uncover my face, nudging at my arms with his nose, tail going ninety miles an hour. Never whines like some dogs do, though. Even when we're out in the far meadow, racing the wind, he'll start to bark and I'll say, "Shhhh, Shiloh!" and he stops right off.

Wish I *could* let him make a little noise. It's not natural, I know, to keep an animal so quiet. But he's *happy*-quiet, not *scared*-quiet. I know that much.

I move my arms off my face after a while and let him rest his paws on my chest, and I'm lying there petting his head and he's got this happy dog-smile on his face. The breeze is blowing cool air in from the west, and I figure I'm about as happy right then as you can get in your whole life.

And then I hear someone say, "Marty." I look up, and there's Ma.

Chapter 9

I CAN'T MOVE. Seems as if they sky's swirling around above me, tree branches going every which way. Ma's face even looks different from down on the ground.

Shiloh, of course, goes right over, tail wagging, but all the steam's gone out of me.

"How long have you had this dog up here?" she asks. Not one trace of a smile on her face.

I sit up real slow and swallow. " 'Bout a week, I guess."

"You've had Judd's dog up here a week, and you told him you didn't know where it was?"

"Didn't say I didn't know. He asked had I seen him, and I said I hadn't seen him in our yard. That much was true."

Ma comes around to the trunk of the pine tree, unfastens the wire that holds the fencing closed, and lets herself in. She crouches down in the soft pine needles and Shiloh starts leaping up on her with his front paws, licking at her face.

I can't tell at first how she feels about him, the way she leans back, away from his dripping tongue. Then I see her hand reach out, with its short, smooth fingers, and stroke him.

"So we've got ourselves a secret," she says at last, and when I hear her say, "we," I feel some better. Not a lot, but some.

"How come you to follow me up here tonight?" I want to know.

Now I can tell for sure her eyes are smiling, but her lips are still set. "Well, I had my suspicions before, but it was the squash that did it."

"The squash?"

"Marty, I never knew you to eat more'n a couple bites of squash in your life, and when you put away a spoonful of that to eat later, I knew for sure it wasn't you doing the eating. And then the way you've been sneaking off every night." She stops stroking Shiloh and turns on me. "I wish you'd told me."

"Figured you'd make me give him back."

"This dog don't belong to you."

"Mine more than Judd's!" I say hotly. "He only paid money for him. I'm the one who loves him."

"That doesn't make him yours. Not in the eyes of the law, it doesn't."

"Well, what kind of law is it, Ma, that lets a man mistreat his dog?"

Ma just sighs then and starts stroking Shiloh's head. Shiloh wiggles a few inches closer to her on his belly, rests his nose against her thigh, tail going *whick, whack, whick, whack.* Finally Ma says, "Your dad don't know about him?"

I shake my head. More silence. Then she says: "I never kept a secret from your dad in the fourteen years we've been married."

"You ain't going to tell him?"

"Marty, I've got to. He ever finds out about this dog and knows I knew but didn't tell him, how could he trust me? If I keep this one secret from him, he'll think maybe there are more."

"He'll make me give him back to Judd, Ma!" I could hear my voice shaking now. "You *know* he will!"

"What else can we do?"

I can feel hot tears in my eyes now and try to keep them from spilling out. I turn my head till they go away. "Judd Travers ever comes here to get his dog, he'll have to fight me to get it."

"Marty . . ."

"Listen, Ma, just for one night, promise you won't tell Dad so I can figure out something."

Can tell she's thinking on it. "You aren't fixing to run off with this dog, are you? Marty, don't you *ever* run away from a problem."

I don't answer, because that very thing crossed my mind.

"I can't promise not to tell your dad tonight if you can't promise not to run off."

"I won't run off," I say.

"Then I won't tell him tonight."

"Or in the morning, neither," I add. "I got to have at least one day to think." Don't know what good it will do, though. Have already thought till my brains are dry.

Ma puts out both hands now and scratches behind Shiloh's ears, and he licks her all up and down her arms.

"His name's Shiloh," I tell her, pleased.

After a while Ma gets up. "You coming back to the house now?"

"In a bit," I answer.

It's hard to say how I feel after she leaves. Glad, in a way, that somebody knows: that I don't have to carry this whole secret on my head alone. But more scared than glad. Have me just one day to think of what to do, and not any closer to an answer than I'd been before. I'd spent all my can money on stuff to feed Shiloh. Only money I have now to my name is a nickel I'd found out by the road. Judd won't sell me Shiloh's spit for a nickel.

My first thought is to give him to somebody else and not tell them whose dog it is, then tell Ma that Shiloh had run off. But that would be two more lies to add to the pack. Word would get out somehow or other, and Judd would see David Howard or Mike Wells walking his dog, and then the war would really start.

All I can think of is to take Shiloh down to Friendly the next day, draw me up a big sign that says FREE: WORLD'S BEST DOG or something, and hold it up along the road to Sistersville, hoping that some stranger driving along will get a warm spot in his heart for Shiloh, stop his car, and take him home. And I won't ask him where home is, neither, so when Ma asks me where the dog is, I can tell her honest I don't know.

When I get back to the house, Dad's just washing up at the pump, using grease to get the oil off his arms. He's yelling and Dara Lynn and Becky, who are playing in the doorway, screen wide open, letting in the moths.

I go inside and ma's putting the dishes away in the kitchen, lifting them out of the drain rack and stacking the plates on the shelf. She's got the radio on and is humming along with a country music song:

> *It's you I wanna come home to,*
> *It's you to bake my bread,*
> *It's you to light my fire,*
> *It's you to share my bed.*

She sort of blushes when she sees me there by the refrigerator, listening to her sing.

I know I'm not going to sleep much that night. I sit on the couch staring at the TV, but not really watching, while Ma gives Becky her bath. Then I wait till Dara Lynn is out of the bathroom so I can take my own bath. Don't know if I soaped up or not. Don't even know if I washed my feet. I go back in the living room, and Ma had my bed made up there on the sofa. The house gets dark, the doors close, and then just the night sounds come from outside.

Know there's a piece of cardboard somewhere out in the shed I can print on. There won't be any trouble getting Shiloh to Friendly, either. I'll put that rope on his collar, and he'll follow along good as anything. We won't take the main road, though, in case Judd's out in his truck. Take every back road I can find.

Then I'll plant myself on the road to Sistersville, holding that sign, Shiloh waiting beside me wondering what it is we're going to do next. What *am* I fixing to do, anyway? Give him to the first car that stops? Don't even know the person driving? Might even be I'll give Shiloh to somebody who'll treat him worse than Judd Travers. Now that Shiloh's come to trust me, here I am getting ready to send him off again. I feel like there's a tank truck sitting on my chest; can't hardly breathe. Got one day to decide what to do with Shiloh, and nothing I think on seems right.

I hear Shiloh making a noise up on the far hill in his pen. Not now, Shiloh! I whisper. You been good as gold all this time. Don't start now. Can it be he knows what I'm fixing to do?

Then I hear a yelp, a loud yelp, then a snarl and a growl, and suddenly the air is filled with yelps, and it's the worst kind of noise you can think of. A dog being hurt.

I leap out of bed, thrust my feet in my sneakers, and with shoelaces flying. I'm racing through the kitchen toward the back door. A light comes on. I can hear Dad's voice saying, "Get a flashlight," but I'm already out on the back porch, then running up the hill.

There are footsteps behind me; Dad's gaining on me. Can hear Shiloh howl like he's being torn in two, and my breath comes shorter and shorter, trying to get there in time.

By the time I reach the pen, Dad's caught up with me, and he's got the flashlight turned toward the noise. The beam searches out the pine tree, the fencing, the lean-to. . . . And then I see this big German shepherd, mean as nails, hunched over Shiloh there on the ground. The shepherd's got blood on his mouth and jaws, and as Dad takes another step forward, it leaps over the fence, same way it got in, and takes off through the woods.

I unfasten the wire next to the pine tree, legs like rubber, hardly holding me up. I kneel down by Shiloh. He's got blood on his side, his ear, a big open gash on one leg, and he don't move. Not an inch.

I bend over, my forehead against him, my hand on his head. He's dead, I know it! I'm screaming inside. Then I feel his body sort of shiver, and his mouth's moving just a little, like he's trying to get his tongue out to lick my hand. And I'm bent over there in the beam of Dad's flashlight, bawling, and I don't even care.

Chapter 10

Dad's beside me, holding the flashlight up to Shiloh's eyes. Shiloh's still alive.

"This Judd Travers's dog?"

I sit back on my heels and nod. Wipe one arm across my face.

Dad looks around. "Take those gunnysacks over there and put 'em in the back of the Jeep," he says, and then, still holding the flashlight in one hand, he slips his arms under Shiloh and picks him up. I can see Shiloh wince and pull back on his leg where it hurts.

The tears are spilling out of my eyes, but Dad can't see 'em in the dark. He can probably tell I'm crying though, 'cause my noes is clogged. "Dad," I say, "*please* don't take him back to Judd! Judd'll take one look at Shiloh and shoot him!"

"Take those gunnysacks to the Jeep like I said," Dad tells me, and I follow behind as we go down the hill. I keep my mouth open to let the breath escape, crying without making a sound. Just like Shiloh.

Ma's watching from inside, the screen all covered with June bugs where they been buzzing about the light. Dara Lynn's up, standing there in her nightshirt, watching.

"What *is* it? What's he got?" Dara Lynn says, pestering Ma's arm.

"A dog," says Ma. And then she calls out, "Ray, is it alive?"

"Just barely," says Dad.

I put the gunnysacks in the Jeep, and Dad carefully lays Shiloh down. Without waiting to ask, I crawl in the Jeep beside Shiloh, and Dad don't say no. He goes in the house for his trousers and his keys, and then we're off.

"I'm sorry, Shiloh," I whisper, over and over, both hands on him so's he won't try to get up. The blood's just pouring from a rip in his ear. "I'm so sorry! Jesus help me, I didn't know Bakers' dog could leap that fence."

When we get to the bottom of the lane, instead of going up the road toward Judd's place, Dad turns left toward Friendly, and halfway around the first curve, he pulls in Doc Murphy's driveway. Light's still on in a window, but I think old doc was in bed, 'cause he come to the door in his pajamas.

"Ray Preston?" he says when he sees Dad.

"I sure am sorry to bother you this hour of the night," Dad says, "but I got a dog here hurt bad, and if you could take a look at him, see if he can be saved, I'd be much obliged. We'll pay. . . ."

"I'm no vet," says Doc Murphy, but he's already standing aside, holding the screen open with one hand so we can carry Shiloh in.

The doc's a short man, round belly, don't seem to practice what he preaches about eating right, but he's got a kind heart, and he lays out some newspapers on his kitchen table.

I'm shaking so hard I can see my own hands tremble as I keep one on Shiloh's head, the other on a front paw.

"He's sure bleeding good, I can tell that," Doc Murphy says. He puts on his stethoscope and listens to Shiloh's heart. Then he takes his flashlight and shines it in the dog's eyes, holding each eye open with his finger and thumb. Finally he looks at the big, ugly wound on Shiloh's hurt leg, torn open right to the bone, the bites around Shiloh's neck, and the ripped ear. I turn my head and sniffle some more.

"I'll do what I can," Doc says. "The thing we got to worry about now is infection. That leg wound is going to take twenty . . . thirty stitches. What happened?"

I figure Dad will answer for me, but he don't—just turns to me. "Marty?"

I swallow. "Big old German shepherd chewed him up."

Doc Murphy goes over the sink and washes his hands. "Baker's dog? Every time that shepherd gets loose, there's trouble." He comes back to the table and takes a big needle out of his bag, fills it full of something. Something to make Shiloh numb, maybe. "This your dog, son?"

I shake my head.

"No?" He looks at me, then at Dad. Dad still won't say nothing, makes me do the talking. While the doc leans over Shiloh and slowly inserts the needle in his side. I get up my nerve.

"It's Judd *Travers*'s," I tell him. I got to start practicing the truth sometime.

"Judd Travers's? This is the dog he's missing? How come you brought it in?"

"I had him," I say.

Doc Murphy sucks in his breath, then lets it out a little at a time—*huh, huh, huh.* "Whew!" he says, and goes on about his work.

Don't know how long we're there in Doc's kitchen, Dad standing over against the wall, arms folded, me with my hand cupped over Shiloh's head while Doc Murphy washes the wounds, dresses them, ands starts stitching the skin back up. Once or twice I feel Shiloh jerk, like it hurts him, but when he lays too still, I don't know if it's because he's numb or if he's dying.

"The next twenty-four hours, we'll know if this dog's going to live," the doc says. "You check with me tomorrow evening; we'll have some idea then. I can keep him here for a day or two, Ray. Then, if he makes it, you can take him on home."

I put my face down near Shiloh's again, my mouth next to his ear. "*Live,* Shiloh, *live!*" I whisper.

Hardest thing in the world is to leave Shiloh there at Doc Murphy's, the way his eyes follow me over to the doorway, the way his muscles move, like he's trying to get up when he sees me leaving. Second hardest thing is to crawl in the Jeep with Dad afterward.

There isn't a word passed between us till we get home. Once Dad turns the motor off, though, and I'm all set to get out, he says, "Marty, what else don't I know?"

"What?" I ask.

"You keeping Judd's dog up there on our hill—got a place for him all built, never letting on. What else you keeping from me?"

"Nothing, Dad!"

"How do I know that's not another lie?"

" 'Cause it's not."

"You saying so don't make it true."

I know then what Ma meant. But its not all so black and white as Dad makes it out to be, neither. And sometimes, when I get mad, it clears my head.

"You would have thought more of me if I'd let that dog wander around till Judd found it again, kick the daylights out of 'im?" I ask. "That what you want me to do, Dad?"

"I want you do what's right."

"What's right?"

For once in my eleven years, I think I have my dad stumped. Leastways, it seems to be thirty . . . forty seconds before he answers:

"You've go to go by the law. The law says a man that pays money for a dog owns that dog. You don't agree with the law, then you work to change it."

"What if there isn't time, Dad? Shiloh could be dead by the time somebody looked into the way Judd treats his dogs."

Dad's voice is sharp: "You think Judd Travers is the only one around here hard-hearted toward his animals? You think he's the only one who starves 'em or kicks 'em or worse? Open your eyes, Marty. *Open your eyes!*" Now Dad turns in his seat, back resting against the door, facing me: "How many times have you walked to the school bus and seen a chained-up dog in somebody's yard? How many times you ever put your mind to whether or not it's happy, its ribs sticking out like handles on the sides? Suddenly you're face-to-face with a dog that pulls at your heart, and you all at once want to change things."

I swallow. "There's got to be a first time," I answer.

Dad sighs. "You're right about that," he says.

I'm pushing my luck, I know. "If Doc Murphy don't tell Judd about Shiloh, can we bring him back here and keep him. I could build him a better pen. Make the fence high enough so the shepherd can't get in."

Dad opens the Jeep door on his side. "No," he says, and gets out.

I get out, too. "Just till Shiloh's better, then? You now how Judd treats anything that don't work right. He'll shoot Shiloh, Dad! I found a dog once before over near Judd's place with a bullet hole in his head. We could at least get Shiloh well. I'm going to pay Doc Murphy's bill. I promise you that. You get all my can money for the next three years, and I'll deliver the county paper, too, if I get the chance. Honest! I promise!"

Dad studies me. "You can keep him here till he's well, that's all. Then we're taking him back to Judd." And he goes in the house.

My heart starts pounding again. *Thumpity, thump. Thumpity thump.* There's still time, I'm thinking. Shiloh's still alive, and I ain't licked yet.

Chapter 11

It's only after I lie back down on the couch that night that I realize what all I've done. To Ma and Dad, for one thing. Ma's still awake. I can see the light in the bedroom as Dad goes on down the hall. And then I hear their voices. Not all of what they say, but enough:

"Ray . . . told you that I just found out about that dog myself . . . ."

". . . secrets from me, you and Marty."

". . . till tomorrow. I would have told you then . . . ."

". . . every day . . . the mail to Judd's place . . . mentions that dog to me, and all the time . . . up on my own property, me not even knowing . . . ."

I bring my arms up against my ears and hold 'em there. So many things going wrong, it's hard to remember anything going right. Doc Murphy knows I've got Judd's dog now, Dad's mad at Ma, and we won't know till tomorrow if Shiloh's even going to make it. Worst of all, I'd brought Shiloh here to keep him from being hurt, and what that German shepherd done to him was probably worse than anything Judd Travers would have brought himself to do, short of shootin' him, anyways. This time, when the tears come again, I don't even fight. Don't even try holding back.

I must have slept through Dad's going off to work the next morning, 'cause when I wake, Becky's standing beside the couch eating a piece of honey toast and breathing on my face. Dara Lynn's already told her about the dog, because she asks right off, "Where's it at, the doggy?"

I sit up and tell her the dog's at Doc Murphy's and we'll find out how he is that afternoon. Then I look in the kitchen at Ma. There's the set look about the lips that means trouble—that means don't mess with her, 'cause she's already in trouble with Dad.

I go outside, pick me a couple wormy peaches, and sit on the stoop, eating at them, spitting out the wormy places.

Dara Lynn comes out and sits beside me. Today she's all kindness.

"Judd Travers don't take care of his dog, Marty, no wonder it come up here," she says, trying to say the right thing. I can tell she's been figuring it all out, from what she could overhear between Ma and Dad and anything else Ma told her.

I take another bite of peach.

"It wasn't like you *stole* him," she says. "That dog come up here on its own."

"Just hush up, Dara Lynn," I say, which I had no business saying. I didn't want to talk to anyone, that's all.

"Well, you could have told me and I wouldn't have told anyone."

"Thanks."

"Ma says we've got to give him back to Judd Travers when he's better."

I get up and start toward the hill to clean up the ground where Shiloh was attacked. See if there's any way I can put some fence wire over the top of the pen to keep out the shepherd.

"What's his name, Marty?" Dara Lynn calls after me.

"Shiloh," I tell her.

I'm only halfway up the hill when I hear a car and turn around. It's Mrs. Howard's car, and David's in it. Soon as he sees me he jumps out— it still moving a little—and comes running toward me.

"I get to stay here today!" he yells, waving a kite he's brought with him. "Everyone else is going to Parkersburg and I didn't want to go."

I look over to where Ma and Mrs. Howard are talking, see Ma nodding her head. I get lonely sometimes up at our house, but today I want to be with that loneliness. Don't want to talk to Dara Lynn, to Becky, to Dad, or even to Ma. If we had a telephone, I'd be calling Doc Murphy every hour. As it is, I have to wait till Dad comes home from work before I can find out about Shiloh. Can't go down there pesterin' Doc, him with patients to see.

"What do you want to do?" I ask David, trying to dig up the least bit of enthusiasm. David and I are in the same grade, even though he's taller and heavier and looks like junior high already.

"Try out this kite over in your meadow," he says.

I lead him around the long way, away from Shiloh's pen, and he doesn't even notice because he's unwrapping his kite, made of silk or something, which one of his relatives brought him.

We stand out in the meadow flying the kite, and I watch the blue-and-yellow-and-green tail whipping around in the breeze, and I'm thinking about Shiloh's tail, the way it wags. You get a dog on your mind, it seems to fill up the whole space. Everything you do reminds you of that dog.

When we bring the kite down later, though, David sees a groundhog, and next thing you know he's after it—the groundhog zigzagging this way and that, David yelling like crazy.

"I'm taking your kite back down to the house, David," I yell when I see him getting near Shiloh's pen.

He goes on running and yelling.

"I'm going to get me a handful of soda crackers. You want to make some peanut-butter-cracker sandwiches?" I call out, trying to get him to follow.

And then his yelling stops. "Hey!" he says.

I know he's found the pen, and I walk over.

"What's this?" David asks. He looks at the blood on the ground. "Hey! What happened here?"

I go over and yank his arm and make him sit down. He's looking at me bug-eyed.

"You listen to me, David Howard," I say. Whenever I say, "David Howard," he knows it's serious. Only did it twice in my life—once when he sat on the paper flowerpot I'd made for Ma at school, and once when he saw me with my pants down in the bathroom. That really made me mad.

But today I'm not mad, I'm serious: "Something awful and terrible happened in there, David, and if you ever tell anyone, even your ma and dad, may Jesus make you blind."

That's the kind of talk my folks can't stand, but I got it from Grandma Preston herself. Ma says Jesus don't go around making anyone blind, but Grandma Preston always used it as a warning and she went to church Sunday morning and evening both.

David's eyes about to pop out of his head. "*What?*" he asks again.

"You know Judd Travers?"

"He was *murdered?*"

"No. But you know the way he's mean to his dogs?"

"He killed one of his dogs in there?"

"*No.* Let me *tell* it, David. You know how he's missing a dog?"

"Yeah?"

"Well, it come up here on its own and I let him stay. I built him a pen and kept him secret and named him Shiloh."

David stares at me, then at the blood in the pen, then back at me again.

"Last night," I tell him, "Baker's German shepherd jumped the fence and tore him up. We took Shiloh to Doc Murphy, and Judd don't know."

David's mouth falls open and hangs there. "Wow!" he says, then says it again.

I tell David how hurt Shiloh was and how we've got to wait till tonight to see how he is, and then we go in his pen together, and David helps me clean up the blood—pull up all the grass with blood stains on it and throw it over the fence into the woods.

It's easier somehow with David helping. With David knowing, even. If it was me by myself, I'd be thinking again and again how this never would have happened if Shiloh could have got away from the shepherd. I look at David and think we're friends for life. Then I think of how there are exactly seven people now who know I have Judd Travers's dog, and it's only a matter of time before somebody lets it out. Probably Becky. She'll warble it to the first person coming up the lane. Did you ever notice how the more a little kid tries not to tell a secret, the sooner it gets out? Nothing that child can do about it. A secret is just too big for a little kid.

What I didn't expect was that at three-thirty, before Dad come home, here's Doc Murphy's car chugging up the lane, and he's got Shiloh in the backseat. I'm standing out by the oak tree with David, taking turns on the bag swing, when I see the car and Shiloh's head raised up in the backseat. I'm over to that car in three seconds flat.

"Shiloh!"

No cry ever sounded so happy as the one that come up out of my throat.

All of us, we're crowing around the car—Ma and Dara Lynn and Becky and David Howard, and all of us are saying, "Shiloh! Here, boy!" and holding out our hands, and Shiloh's trying to lick everything in sight.

"Patient recovered faster than I thought he would," Doc says, getting his big belly out from behind the steering wheel and standing up. "So I figured I'd bring him on over myself."

And then, to Mother, "Had patients coming in and out today, and don't know that I wanted them to see the dog."

She nodded.

"I'm going to pay for this, Doc Murphy," I tell him. "You send the bill to Dad and he'll pay it, but then I'm payin' him."

"Well, son, that's a generous thing to do, with a dog not even yours," he says.

"Is he all well now?"

"No. Not by a long shot. Think it's going to take a couple weeks to heal, and I can't promise you he'll walk without a limp. But I got him sewn back up and full of antibiotics. If you can keep him quiet for a few days and off that leg, I think he'll pull through just fine."

If Ma was mad at me before, she's not now, not the way Shiloh's licking her all over both arms, getting a quick lick in at her face every time she bends close. Becky's sticking her hand out for Shiloh to lick, and when he does, she squeals and pulls back. Shiloh's tail going like crazy.

It's like a welcome-home party. Ma has me bring in this cardboard box from the shed and we put an old pillow in the bottom of it and cover it with a clean sheet, and Doc Murphy lays Shiloh down inside it.

Shiloh seems to know he can't walk too good, because as soon as he tries to stand up, he sits back down again and licks at his leg.

I'm glad Shiloh's back, I'm glad he's going to get better, and that we can keep him till he's well. But the more I sit there petting his head, feeling his happiness, the more I know I can't give him up. I won't.

Chapter 12

Sure seems strange having Shiloh in the house that night, after trying so hard to keep him secret. Strange, too, the way Ma takes to him. Seems like she can't hardly pass his box next to the stove without reaching down to pet him, making low sympathy noises in her throat, way she does when Dara Lynn or Becky or me gets sick.

Dad don't say much. He come home to find Shiloh there, he just stands off to one side, listening to what Doc Murphy said about him; he don't get close enough for Shiloh to take a lick.

But when supper's over and I go off to the bathroom to brush my teeth, I peek back through the doorway, and Dad's over by Shiloh's box, letting him lick his plate clean. Dad crouches there a minute or two, scratching all down Shiloh's back and up again.

What I'm figuring, see, is by the time Shiloh's better, everybody will love him so much they just can't let him go—even Dad. I'm hoping Dad will go over to see Judd Travers, make him an offer for Shiloh, and then he'll be ours. The trouble with this kind of thinking, though, is we don't have the money.

I'll probably be through junior high school, almost, before I earn enough to pay Doc Murphy's bill. To buy Shiloh from Judd, even if Judd's willing to sell, I'd have to collect aluminum cans all through high school, too. Can't make very much with cans. I try to think about what other kind of work I can do that would pay me more, but except for delivering the county paper on Friday afternoons, nothing else comes to mind. And somebody's got that job already.

It's sort of like Shiloh's there and he's not. In the next couple of days, everybody's pettin' him every chance they get. Becky feeds him the crusts of her toast—breaks off little bits, and shrieks every time she feels Shiloh's mouth slurp them out of her fingers.

Ma's putting up beans in jars, and all the while she hums to Shiloh like he's a baby in a cradle, not a dog in a box. Dara Lynn's got an old hairbrush, and she just can't seem to brush that dog enough. Even Dad sits down one evening and gets out every tick Shiloh's got on him. Takes a little dab of turpentine and rubs it on the tick's rear end, and the tick backs out of Shiloh's skin mighty quick.

The thing that makes it seem like Shiloh's *not* there is that nobody except me and Dara Lynn and Becky talks about him. Ma and Dad don't even once mention his name out loud, as though saying it makes him ours, which he ain't. As though if you don't talk about him, maybe he'll disappear as quietly as he came that day in the rain.

What everyone's waiting for, I guess, is something to happen. Every day Shiloh's getting a little stronger. Two days after Doc Murphy brought him here, Shiloh's up limping around on his bad leg. Ma puts some papers beside his box for him to do his business on, but he won't, so for the first couple days I pick him up, carry him out to the yard, and after he's done his business there, I bring him in again. But now he's pushing open the back screen himself and going down into the yard, then comin' back and tapping on the screen with one paw, so we'll let him in. Somebody, sometime, is bound to see him. Becky, sometime, bound to say something. Even David Howard, when his ma came to pick him up the other day, opens his mouth right off and says something about Shiloh.

"Who's Shiloh?" she asks, and David realizes he's let it slip.

"Old stray cat," he says, and now I've got David lying.

Worse part about having Shiloh here in the house where I can play with him anytime I like is that it's hard to leave him when I go out collecting cans. But I've got to earn money now more than ever, so each day, when Shiloh takes his long nap, I set out with my plastic garbage bag hanging out one jeans' pocket.

One day I walk all the way to Friendly and ask at the grocery, where the county paper is dropped, if they'll put in my name as a carrier. Mr. Wallace says he'll turn my name in, but he's already got six names ahead of me, and one of 'em is a grown man with a car. Don't see how I can match that.

I study the bulletin board at the back of the store where people put up notices. Stand on one foot and then the other reading the whole danged board, and seems like everybody got something to sell, or want to be hired, nobody wants to buy. Only two jobs listed, one for an appliance salesman and some woman who wants her house painted.

Mr. Wallace sees me looking at the board, and he comes over and takes down the notice about a woman wanting her house painted.

"That's already taken," he tells me.

That night, while we finish supper, Shiloh's going around the table, putting his nose in everyone's lap, looking mournful, waiting for somebody to slip him something to eat. I can tell Ma and Dad's trying their best not to laugh. Ma won't let us feed him at the table.

What I'm dying to ask Dad is did he tell Judd Travers about his dog being here. Dad don't mention it so I don't ask. Maybe I don't want to know, I tell myself.

And then, just as Ma's dishing up a peach cobbler that we're going to eat hot with milk, I hear a sound outside that makes my bones feel like icicles inside me.

Shiloh hears it too, and I know right away it's what I think it is, because Shiloh sticks his tail between his legs, and puts his belly low to the floor, and climbs back into his box.

Ma and Dad look at Shiloh. They look at each other. Then there's the slam of a truck door outside, footsteps on the ground, footsteps on the porch, and a *rap, rap, rap* at the back door. Everybody stops eating, like we was all froze to death in our chairs.

Dad gets up and turns on the porch light, and there he is, Judd Travers, looking as mean and nasty as I ever seen him look. He don't even ask can he come in; just opens the screen and steps inside.

"Ray Preston," he says, "somebody told me you got my dog."

Dad's looking serious. He nods and points toward the box by the stove. "Over there, Judd, but he's hurt, and we've been taking care of him for you."

Judd stares at Shiloh and then at Dad. "Well, I'll be danged," he says, almost softly. "Somebody knows my dog is missing, takes him in, and don't even have the decency to tell me."

"We *were* going to tell you," Dad says, and he's looking straight at Judd. "Nobody wants to hear his dog's been hurt, though, and we wanted to make sure he was going to pull through." Then he turns to me. "Marty," he says, "you want to tell Mr. Travers how his dog come to be here?"

He knows I don't. He knows I'd rather swim a river full of crocodiles than face Judd Travers. But it's my story to tell, not Dad's, and he always did make us face up to what we'd done.

"Your dog come over here twice because you been mistreatin' it," I say, and my voice don't sound near as strong as Dad's. Sort of quavery. I clear my throat and go on: "So second time it come over, I built it a pen up in the woods and Dad didn't know it, and that German shepherd of Baker's got in and fought Shiloh."

"Fought who?"

"The beagle. Shiloh, that's what I've been callin' him. And Shiloh got hurt bad. It was my fault for not making the fence higher. We took him to Doc Murphy and he patched him up."

Judd Travers is still staring around the room like he never saw the likes of us before. Finally he lets out his breath through his teeth and slowly shakes his head: "And I got to find out all this from Doc Murphy?"

I couldn't believe Doc would go tell him.

"Somebody goes to the doc the other day and sees a beagle lying out on his back porch. Tells me about it later. Says he thinks maybe the dog's mine. So I ride over to Doc's this evening and he tells me it was you who brought him in."

Judd walks across the kitchen, and at the thud of each footstep, Shiloh huddles down farther and farther in the box, like maybe he can make himself disappear. His whole body is shaking. Ma sees it, I know, because she watches for a minute, then turns her face away quick.

Judd stares down at Shiloh—at his bandage and the shaved place where he's all stitched up—the rip on his ear. "Look what you done to my *dog!*" he yells at me, eyes big and angry. I swallow. Nothin' I can say to that.

Travers squats down by the box. He puts out his hand, and Shiloh leans away, like he's going to be hit. If that don't prove the way he treats 'em, I don't know what would, but Judd's saying, "I never mistreated my dogs. This one was shy when I got him, that's all. I sure never caused him an injury like this one. Wouldn't never have happened if you'd brought him back like I told you." I close my eyes.

When I open 'em again, Judd's putting his hand on Shiloh's head, roughlike, sort of patting him, and you can tell he ain't got that much practice being kind. Still, hard to prove Shiloh wasn't mistreated *before* he got to Judd's. How do you go about proving something like that?

"It was wrong of Marty to pen up your dog, Judd, and we've already talked about that," Dad says. "He's the one who's going to pay Doc Murphy for patching him up, and soon as the dog is strong, we'll drive him over to your place. Why don't you let us keep him until then, in case he needs more care?"

Judd stands up again and looks at me. I stare back, but I don't say nothing.

And then Ma can't take it anymore. She says, "Judd, Marty's got awful attached to that dog, and we'd like to know how much you want for it. Maybe we can scrape up the money to buy him."

Judd looks at her like she's talking some kind of nonsense, like we are all getting crazier by the minute.

"That dog's not for sale," he says. "Paid good money to get me a hunting dog, and he could be one of the best I've had. You want to keep and feed him till he's better, okay with me. It's you that got him all tore up, and you paying the bill. But I want him back by Sunday."

Screen door slams again, truck starts up, and then he's gone.

Chapter 13

I'M BACK TO not sleeping again. Everything I can think of to try, I've already thought on and turned down. Even thought of Dad and me driving to Middlebourne and going to the county courthouse to report a man who's mean to his dogs, thinking maybe they wouldn't let Judd have Shiloh back again. Dad says that's where we'd have to go, all right, but how am I going to prove it about Judd? Think about that, he says.

I been thinking about it. Do I really suppose they'd send an investigator all the way out from Middlebourne to see about a man said to kick his dogs? And if they did, do I think Judd's going to tell the man yes, indeed, he does kick them? Do I think the investigator's going to hide out in the bushes near Judd Travers's place for a week just to see for himself?

Tyler County hasn't hardly got the money to investigate reports of children being kicked, Dad says, much less dogs. Even if I told the animal-rights people that I found a dog with a bullet hole in its head up near Judd's house, don't prove that Judd was the one who killed it.

I go out to talk to Dad about it some more while he's chopping wood, and he just says, "Son, it's hard, I know, but sometimes you just got to do what has to be done. It's Judd's dog and there's no getting around it."

Ma tries to make me feel better. She says at least I brought some joy and kindness into the life of dog that never had any before, and that Shiloh will never forget me. But that even makes it worse. Wish he *could* forget. Keep thinking of how Shiloh's going to look at me when we drive him over to Judd's, and my eyes fill up again. Becky, she's been crying, too. So has Dara Lynn. The one good thing about it now is that the whole family loves Shiloh and we can talk about him out loud, but there's not one thing we can do. Three more days and we have to give him up.

I walk down to Friendly on Friday to talk with David Howard. David feels almost as bad as I do. I hardly finish telling about

Shiloh and he's got tears in his eyes already. David Howard's thirty pounds heavier and bigger than me, and he still don't care who sees him cry.

"I been thinking, David," I say. "You got relatives in Ohio, don't you?"

He nods.

"You think any of them would take Shiloh? Could you call 'em up and ask could they drive down here tomorrow and take him back with them, and I'll tell Judd we let Shiloh out one day and he never come back?" More lies.

But David's shaking his head already. "It's only Uncle Clyde and Aunt Pat, and she's allergic to dogs. They had one once and had to give him up."

On the way back home, I'm thinking about some place really good I could hide that dog. The old gristmill, maybe, up by the bridge. The door's padlocked, but it don't take much to get in, 'cause the top of the building's open where some of the roof's blown away. I bet I could hide Shiloh in there for ten years and he'd never make a sound. But what kind of life is that? Couldn't never take him anywhere except after dark. Even then, he'd be so close to Judd's place, the other dogs would probably sniff him out.

Slowly the minutes and hours of Friday tick by, then it's Saturday, and our last day with Shiloh. We give him every little treat we can think of, a wonder we don't make him sick, and after supper we sit out on the back porch like we usually do. Becky and Dara Lynn are rolling around in the grass, and Shiloh limps out there to join in the fun. I show Becky how if you lay down on your stomach with your arms up over your face, Shiloh will work to turn you over. Both girls have to try it, and Shiloh does just like I said, trying his best to get those girls up on their feet.

"If Becky ever fell in the creek, I'll bet Shiloh would pull her out," Ma says.

"If I ever saw a snake, I'll bet Shiloh would kill it for me," says Dara Lynn.

I got a sadness inside me growing so big I feel I'm about to bust. That night I sleep a little bit, wake a bit, sleep a bit, wake some more. About dawn, however, I know what I got to do.

I get up quiet as can be. Soon as Shiloh hears me, of course, he's out of his box.

"Shhh, Shiloh," I say, my finger to my lips. He watches me a moment, then crawls back in his box, good as ever.

I dress, pull on my sneakers, take me slice of bread from the loaf on the counter and a peach off the tree in the yard. Then I take the shortcut through the east woods toward Judd Travers's.

It's the only thing left to do. I'd talked to Dad, to Ma, to David, and nobody's got any more idea what to do than they did before. What I'm fixing to do is talk to Judd Travers straight and tell him I'm not going to give Shiloh back.

Rehearse my lines so often I can say 'em by heart. What I don't know, though, is what Judd's going to say—what he's going to do. I'll tell him he can beat me, punch me, kick me, but I'm not going to give that dog up. I'll buy Shiloh from Judd, but if he won't sell and comes to get him, I'll take Shiloh and head out in the other direction. Only way he can get his dog back is to take me to court, and then I'll tell the judge how Judd treats his animals.

Halfway through the woods, I'm thinking that what I'm about to do could get my dad in a whole lot of trouble. Around here it's serious business when you got a quarrel with your neighbor and you got to carry it as far as the law. Folks ain't that fond of Judd, and most of 'em likes my dad, but when it comes to taking a man's property, I figure they'll side with Judd. I'm not makin' life one bit easier for my parents or Dara Lynn or Becky, but I just can't give up Shiloh without a fight.

Will he shoot me? That thought crosses my mind, too. Some kid got shot down in Mingo County once. Easy as pie for Judd Travers to put a bullet hole in my head, say he didn't see me. I got my feet pointed toward Judd Travers's place, though, and they ain't about to turn back.

Still so early in the morning the mist is rising up out of the ground, and when I come to a stretch of field, looks like the grass is steaming. Sky's light, but the sun hasn't showed itself yet. You live in hill country, it takes a while for the sun to rise. Got to scale the mountains first.

I'm practicing being quiet. What I hope is to get to Judd's house before he's wide awake, take him by surprise. He sees me coming a half mile off, without Shiloh, he's likely to figure what I got to say and have his answer ready. I want to be sitting there on his porch the moment he gets out of bed.

A rabbit goes lickety-split in front of me, then disappears. I went out hunting with Dad once, and he said that when you first scare up a rabbit, it hops a short way, then stops and looks back. That's when you got to freeze. Can't move nothing but your eyeballs, Dad says. What you have to look for is that shiny black dot—the rabbits' eye. If you look for the whole rabbit, you almost never see him because he blends into the scenery.

So I don't move a muscle and look for the shiny black dot. And there it is. I wonder what's going on inside that rabbit—if its heart's pounding fierce. No way I could tell it I wasn't going to do it harm. So I go on, back into the second stretch of woods, heading for that second field.

I'm just about to come out of the trees when I stop dead still again, for right there in the meadow is a deer, a young doe. She's munching on something, and every so often she stops, looks up, then goes on eating again.

Hardest thing in the world for me to see how anybody could shoot an animal like that. Then I think of a couple winters we hardly had any meat on our table, and I guess I can see how a father with three kids could shoot a deer. Hope I never have to, though. I'm just about to step out into the meadow, when *crack!*

It's the sound of a rifle. It splits the air and echoes back against the hills.

The doe takes out across the meadow, heading for the woods. Its front legs rear up, then its back legs as it leaps, its tail a flash of white.

Crack!

The rifle sounds again, and this time the deer goes down.

I can't move. One part of me wants to go to the deer, the other part knows that somebody's out there with a rifle shooting deer out of season. And before I can decide whether to go on or turn back, out of the woods on the other side steps Judd Travers, rifle in hand.

Chapter 14

HE'S WEARING this army camouflage shirt, a brown cap, and the weirdest grin that could fit on a human face.

"Whooeee!" he says, holding the rifle up with one hand as he plows through the weeds. "I got 'er! Whooeee!"

I know he wasn't out shooting rabbits and happened to get a doe instead, because he doesn't have his hounds with him; Judd Travers had gone out that morning with the clear intention of getting himself a deer. I also know that if the game warden finds out about it, Judd's in big trouble, 'cause the deer he shot out of season wasn't even a buck.

He slogs over through waist-high weeds to where the doe lays. Bending over, he looks at her, walks around a little piece, then says "Whooeee!" again, soft-like.

That's when I come out of the woods. He's got his back to me now, his hands on the doe's front legs, trying to see can he pull her himself. Drags her a little way and stops. And when he looks up again, I'm right beside him.

He whirls around. "Where'd you come from?" he says.

"Was on my way over to see you," I tell him, and for the first time, standing next to Judd Travers, I feel taller than I really am.

He looks at me a moment like he don't know if he's glad I'm there or not. Then I guess he figures me being there, only a kid, don't matter. "Look what I got!" he says. "Found her eatin' at my garden this morning, and I chased her over here."

"That's a lie," I say. "I was back in the woods watching her eat. She was comin' down from the hills the other way. You went out deer huntin' for anything you could get."

"Well, supposing I did!" says Judd Travers, and he hates me worse'n snot.

"Deer ain't in season, that's what," I answer. "There's a two-hundred-dollar fine for killing a doe."

Judd Travers is staring at me like he's about to crack me across the mouth. Way we're raised around here, children don't talk back to grown folks. Don't hardly talk much at all, in fact. Learn to listen, keep your mouth shut, let the grown folks do the talking. And here I am, shooting off my mouth at five-thirty in the morning to a man holding a rifle. Am I crazy or what?

"Not unless the game warden finds out, there's not," Judd says. "And who's going to tell him? You?"

All at once I realize I got Judd Travers right where I want him. One way you look at it, it's my duty to report a killed doe. The way folks up here look at it, though, that's snitching. And if I *might* could tell, but bargain not to, it's something else again: It's blackmail. But, like I said, I'd got to the place I'd do most anything to save Shiloh.

"Yeah," I say, my heart pounding like crazy. "I'll tell. There's a free number to call." There is, too. It's on Dad's hunting regulation papers. Boy, I sure didn't know I was going to step into all this when I come up here this morning.

Now Judd's looking at me good, eyes narrowed down to little slits. "Your pa put you up to this?"

"No. This is me talking."

"Well, ain't you something now! And who's to believe you?"

"I'll get the game warden up here, show him the spot the doe was hit, the blood, and when he finds the deer at your place, he'll believe me." The words are coming out quicker than I can think, almost.

"I'll tell him he was eatin' my garden."

"And I'll say different. The new game warden won't make any allowance even if the deer *was* eating your garden. You just don't shoot deer out of season no way. 'Specially a doe."

Now Judd's really angry, and his words come at me like bees. "What you trying to do, boy? Start up trouble? You think I can't put you in your place mighty quick?"

"So what you going to do?" I ask. "Shoot me?"

Travers is so surprised his jaw drops. But I'm cooking now. Nothing can stop me. Braver than I ever been in my life.

"Going to shoot me like that dog I found up here six months back with a bullet in his head?"

Travers stares some more.

"I know whose bullet that was, Judd, and I told Dad, and if folks find me up here with a bullet in me, Dad'll know whose bullet that is, too." I can't hardly believe the words that's coming out of my mouth. Been scared most my life of Judd Travers, and here I am, half his size, talking like a grown person. It's because I know Shiloh's still got a chance.

"So what you waiting for?" Judd says finally. "Go get the game warden." And when I don't move, he says, "Come off it, Marty. Here. You take one of those legs, I'll take another, we'll drag it to my place, and I'll give you half the meat. And don't tell me your ma won't be glad to get it."

"I don't want the meat. I want Shiloh."

Now Judd's really surprised and whistles through his teeth. "Boy, you just come up here to set me up, didn't you?"

"Didn't have an idea in this world you was out with your rifle," I tell him, and that's one of the first truths I told in two weeks. "I come up here because it's Sunday, the day you said to bring your dog back, and I wanted you to know you got to fight me first to get him. Now I'm telling you I mean to keep him, and you expect to keep that deer without a fine, you'll make the trade."

"Whoa!" says Travers. "That's no kind of trade at all! If I *hadn't* got me a deer this morning, what would you have bargained with then?"

I didn't have an answer to that because I hadn't been thinking about a deal. Judd had already said he wouldn't sell Shiloh.

Judd's eyes narrow down even more till it almost looks like he's asleep. "I just bet you *would* tell the game warden, too."

"Jesus' name, I would."

"And you're sayin' if I let you keep my huntin' dog, you're going to keep this deer a secret?"

I begin to see now I'm no better than Judd Travers—willing to look the other way to get something I want. But the something is Shiloh.

"Yes, I will," I tell him, not feeling all that great about it.

"Well, you got to do more than that, boy, because I paid thirty-five dollars for that dog, and I want forty to let him go."

For the first time, I see a thin ray of hope that maybe he'll let me buy Shiloh. "I'll get you the money somehow, by and by," I promise.

"I don't want the money by and by. I want it now. And you haven't got it now, you work for me and pay it off."

You make a deal with Judd Travers and you're only eleven years old, you take what you can get. But all I'm thinking is *dog*.

"You got a bargain," I tell Judd, and now my feet want to dance, my face wants to smile, but I don't dare let the delight show through.

"You listen here," says Judd. "I'll pay you two dollars an hour, and that comes to twenty hours to earn forty dollars. And the work ain't easy."

"I'll do it," I say.

"Beginning now," says Judd, and I can tell he's gettin' a bit edgy that someone else might come through the field, wondering about those rifle shots, and see how he got a doe. "Help me get this deer to my trailer."

I'm so glad to be gettin' Shiloh, I can hardly think straight. But I'm thinkin' straight enough as I help drag that doe to Judd's to know that by lettin' him get away with this, I'm putting other deer in danger. He kill this one out of season, he'll figure maybe he can kill some more. To save Shiloh, I'm making it harder for deer. I swallow. All I got to do, though, is think of the way he'd look at me, I ever give him back to Judd, and then I get on with my job.

When we get to the trailer at last, we carry the deer around to the three-sided shed Judd's got in his backyard. First thing Judd does is bleed the doe, keep the meat from spoilin'. Then he goes out and messes up the tracks with is foot, kicking up the grass where we'd matted it down, and covering the trail of blood with dust.

"I git home from work every day at three," Judd says, "and I want you here when I pull up. You work for me two hours a day, five days a week. I want that wood back there stacked. I want the weeds cut and the grass mowed. I want my beans picked, the corn hoed. . . . Whatever I think of to be done, that's what you do. And I want you here startin' tomorrow."

"I'll be here," I say. "But I want it in writing that after I do my twenty hours' work for you , Shiloh belongs to me."

Travers grunts and goes in his trailer. He comes out with piece of grocery sack and the words "Beagle hunting dog to Marty Preston for twenty hours work. J. Travers."

It occurs to me suddenly that maybe after I do the work, he'll try to pay me off with one of his other dogs.

"Write 'Shiloh,' " I tell him.

He gives me a pained look and crosses out "beagle," writes "Shiloh" in its place, but don't spell it right. Leaves off the "h" at the end.

I take the paper and put it in my pocket. "I'll be here tomorrow," I say.

"And you ever tell *anyone* about this deer, boy, you're going to be more'n sorry you opened your lips."

"You got my word," I say, which, considering all the lying I'd been doing lately, didn't seem like it amounted to much. It did, though.

I walk away from Judd's trailer in a sort of zigzag line, half expecting a bullet in my back any moment, even though I'm pretty sure he wouldn't. Soon as I'm out of sight, though, I race through the woods, heart going *thumpity-thump*. Can't keep the smile back no longer.

Shiloh's mine! The words keep coming back again and again. He's safe!

Should feel even more joyful, though. Thought once if I could just get Shiloh for my own, it would be the finest day of my life. In a way it is, in a way it isn't.

Could be Judd gave in 'cause he couldn't think of nothing else at the moment to do. Said I could have Shiloh just 'cause he needed some help with that deer. Could be that once he got rid of the evidence, he'd tell me to go ahead and get the warden, that I wasn't to have the dog. Could even say he never wrote that on the grocery sack, that I'd wrote it myself.

I don't think so, though. What worries me most is that Judd could go through with the bargain, give Shiloh to me, but then someday, when Shiloh's running free in the woods by himself, Judd might put a bullet in his head, just to spite me.

Chapter 15

CLOSER I GET to home, though, the bigger the grin on my face, and when I burst in the kitchen, I got a smile from ear to ear.

Dad's having his coffee and Ma's in the living room listening to the Sunday morning service by Brother Jonas. She watches him every Sunday at seven, which tells me what time it is already.

"Where you been?" says Dad, and I can tell Ma's paying attention, too. "You up and gone, we got to worrying."

I slide into my chair and almost have to push my cheeks in the keep the smile from going all the way around my head.

"Went to see Judd Travers," I say, still breathless, "and I'm buying his dog."

Ma gets up and comes to the kitchen doorway. "What?"

"Thought he wasn't selling," says Dad, looking at me hard.

"He wasn't, but I talked him into it. He needs help around his place, and he says if I work hard for him for twenty hours, at two dollars a hour, that will pay the forty dollars he wants for Shiloh."

Ma's smile getting broader by the minute. "I don't *believe* it!" she says. "Shiloh's yours?"

"Not yet, but he will be, and we don't have to take him over to Judd's." Before I can get the last word out, she's got her arms around me, squeezing the breath from my chest, almost.

I think Shiloh can smell Judd Travers on me. He can smell the deer's blood, too; I know by the way he sniffs my shoes. But finally he just can't stand it no more. He's joyful I'm back, and he's lickin' me, welcoming me home.

But Dad's still studying my face. "I can't figure it, Marty. Judd seemed pretty definite about keepin' that dog. What was said between you?"

I really didn't want to lie no more. If I tell Ma and Dad everything except about the deer, that's lying by omission. Ma says: not telling the whole truth. But if I tell about the deer after promising Judd I wouldn't, then I would have lied to Judd. Rather lie to Judd than my folks, but I figure it this way: Dad wouldn't report Judd even if *he* saw him shoot a doe out of season, because that's the way it's always been around here. That don't necessarily make it right, of course, but with him feeling that way, nothing's going to change if I *do* tell him about Judd and the deer, and because I promised not to, I don't. Right now, the most important thing to me is Shiloh.

"Told him I wasn't going to give Shiloh back no matter what," I tell Dad.

They are sure staring at me now, him and Ma.

"You said that to Judd Travers?" Dad asked, scooting back in his chair.

"Only thing left to say. Only thing I could think of to do I hadn't tried already. Was going to tell him he could take me to court, and I'd tell the judge how he kicked his dogs. But didn't have to go that far. Guess he needs help around his place."

Ma turns to Dad. "You know, I think it's because Shiloh was hurt. I think he figures that dog's never going to be what it was, and that's why he was willing to let it go. Figured he got rid of a lame dog, and the best of the bargain, too."

"That's what I figure," I say.

And at last Dad begins to smile. "So we got ourselves a new member of the family," he tells me, and that's about the nicest thing I heard said in this house in my life.

Then Becky and Dara Lynn wakes up, sad faced 'cause they think we got to take Shiloh over to Judd's. I tell 'em the news, and Dara Lynn, she starts dancing. Becky joins in, whirling herself around, and then Shiloh, smiling his dog-smile, everybody whooping and carrying on.

Ma turns off the TV and makes waffles, with a big pat of margerine in the center of each one and hot homemade brown-sugar syrup filling the plates. She even makes a waffle for Shiloh. We're going to make that dog sick if we're not careful.

"Now all we got to worry about is how we can afford to feed him as well as ourselves," Dad says finally. "But there's food for the body and food for the spirit. And Shiloh sure enough feeds our spirit."

We about pet Shiloh to death. Everytime he turns around, someone's got a hand on him somewheres. I take him out for his first gentle run since he got hurt, and once up on the hill, him running free, the good feeling inside me grows bigger and bigger and I have to let it out. I hunch my shoulder and go, "Heeeowl!"

Shiloh jumps and looks at me.

"Heeeowl!" I go again, out of joy and jubilation, the way they do in church. And suddenly Shiloh joins in with a bark. A pitiful kind of bark, like he's got to be taught how, but it's a happy bark, and he's learnin'.

Only bit of sadness left in me is for the deer. Wondering, too, about whose business it is when someone breaks the law. Wonder if Dad wouldn't never tell on Judd no matter what he done. Bet he would. There's got to be times that what one person does is everybody's business.

Monday afternoon at three o'clock, I'm waiting on Judd's porch when he pulls up. All his dogs is chained out to the side of the house, and they get to barkin' like crazy. I don't try to get near 'em, 'cause a chained dog can be mean. I've already restacked Judd's woodpile, but he wants me to do it again, put the big pieces here, the little ones there. He is looking mean and grumpy, like maybe he's disgusted with himself for lettin' me have that dog so easy.

When I finish the woodpile, Judd hands me the hoe. "You see that garden?"

I nod.

"You see that corn? I want the dirt chopped up so fine I can sift it through my fingers," he tells me.

Now I see what he's getting at. He's going to make it so there's no way I can please him. I'll put in my twenty hours and he'll tell me my work wasn't no good, he wants his dog back.

I hoe till I got blisters on both hands, sweat pouring down my back. Wish I could do my work in the early morning before the sun's so fierce. But I don't complain. I take off my T-shirt finally, wrap it around my head to keep the sweat out of my eyes, and I keep on. Shoulders so red I know they'll hurt worse'n anything the next morning, and they do.

Next afternoon, Judd sets me to scrubbing down the side of his trailer and his porch, shining up the windows, raking the yard. He sits on a folding chair in the shade, drinking a cold beer. Don't offer me nothing, even water. I hate him more than the devil. My mouth so dry it feels like fur.

Third day, though, he puts out a quart jar of water for me when I go to pick his beans. I bend over them rows so long, dropping the beans into a bucket, I think I'm going to be bent for life. When I'm through, Judd sort of motions me to the porch, like I can sit there if I want while I drink my water.

I almost fall onto that porch, glad to be in the shade.

"Looks like you got yourself some blisters," he says.

"I'm okay," I tell him, and take another long drink.

"How's Shiloh?" he asks. First time he's called the dog by that name.

"He's doing fine. Still got a limp, but he eats good."

Judd lifts his beer to his lips. "Would have been a good hunting dog if I could just have kept him home," he says. "The other dogs never run off."

I think about that awhile. "Well," I say finally, "each one is different."

"That's the truth. Kick one and he just goes under the porch for an hour. Kick another, he goes off and don't come back."

I'm trying my best to think what to say to that. Like how come he has to kick them at all? Then I figure nobody likes to be preached at, no matter how much he needs it, least of all Judd Travers, who is thirty years old if he's a day.

"Some dogs, it just makes 'em mean when you kick 'em," I say, finally. "Other dogs, it makes 'em scared. Shiloh got scared."

"Never beat my dogs with a stick," Judd goes on. "Never did that in my life."

I don't say anything right away. Finally though, I ask, "How *your* dogs doing?"

"Rarin' to go out rabbit hunting," Judd says. We look over at his three dogs, all pullin' at their chains and snarlin' at each other. "That biggest dog, now," Judd goes on. "He's the loudest squaller I got. I can tell from his racket whether he's following a fresh track or an old one, if he's runnin' a ditch, swimmin', or treed a coon."

"That's pretty good," I say.

"Littlest one, he's nothin' but a trashy dog—he'll run down most anything 'cept what I'm after. Hope the others'll learn him something. And the middle dog, well, she gives a lot of mouth, too. Even barks at dead trees." The dogs were fighting now, and Judd throw his Pabst can at 'em. "You-all shut up!" he yells. "Hush up!"

The can hits the biggest dog, and they all scatter.

"Don't much like bein' chained," Judd says.

"Guess nobody would," I tell him.

I put in ten hours that week, meaning I make up twenty of the dollars I owe him; got one more week to go. When I leave of an afternoon for Judd's, Shiloh goes with me just so far, then he gets to whining and turns back. I'm glad he won't go on with me. Don't want him anywhere near Judd Travers.

Monday of the second week it seem like Judd's out to break my back or my spirit or both. This time he's got me spittin' wood. I got to roll a big old piece of locust wood over to the stump in his side yard, drive a wedge in it, then hit the wedge with a sledgehammer, again and again till the wood falls apart in pieces to fit his wood stove. Then another log and another.

I can hardly get the sledgehammer up over my head, and when I bring it down, my arms is so wobbly my aim ain't true. Almost drop the hammer. This ain't a job for me, and if Dad saw what Judd was makin' me do, he'd tell him it wasn't safe.

But Judd's out to teach me a lesson, and I'm out to teach him one. So I keep at it. Know it takes me twice as long as Judd to split that wood, but I don't stop. And all the while, Judd sits on his porch, drinking his beer, watching me sweat. Sure does his heart good, I can tell.

Then he says somethin' that almost stops my heart cold. Laughs and says. "Boy, you sure are puttin' in a whole lot of work for nothin'." I rest my back for a moment, wipe one arm across my face. "Shiloh's somethin'," I tell him.

"You think you're goin' to get my dog just 'cause you got some handwritin' on a piece of paper?" Judd laughs and drinks some more. "Why, that paper's not good for anything but to blow your nose on. Didn't have a witness."

I look at Judd. "What you mean?"

"You don't even know what's legal and what's not, do you? Well, you show a judge a paper without a witness's signature, he'll laugh you right out of the courthouse. Got to have somebody sign that he saw you strike a bargain." Judd laughs some more. "And nobody here but my dogs."

I feel sick inside, like I could maybe throw up. Can't think of what to do or say, so I just lift the sledgehammer again, go on splittin' the wood.

Judd laughs even harder. "What are you, boy? Some kind of fool?" And when I don't answer, he says, "What you breakin' your back for?" "I want that dog," I tell him and raise the sledgehammer again.

That night when I'm sittin' out on the porch with Ma and Dad, Shiloh on my lap, I check it out. "What's a witness?" I say.

"Somebody who knows the Lord Jesus and don't mind tellin' about it," says Ma.

"No, the other kind."

"Somebody who sees something happen and signs that it's true," Dad says. "What you got in mind now, Marty?"

"You make a bargain with somebody, you got to have a witness?" I ask, not answering.

"If you want it done right and legal, I suppose you do."

I can't bear to have Dad know I was so stupid I made an agreement with Judd Travers without a witness.

"What you thinking on?" Dad asks again, hunching up his shoulders while Ma rubs his back.

"Just thinking on how you sell something, is all. Land and stuff."

Dad looks at me quick. "You're not trying to sell of some of my land for that dog, are you?"

"No," I tell him, glad I got him off track. But I sure am worried. Every trace of that deer's gone now. Don't know what Judd done with the meat—rented him a meat locker somewhere, maybe. But there's no bones around, no hide. I report him now, I can't prove a thing.

Next day Judd Travers calls me dumb. Sees me waiting for him on his steps and says I must have a head as thick as a coconut; didn't he already tell me that the paper wasn't worth nothing?

I just look straight through him. "You and me made a bargain," I says, "and I aim to keep my part of it. What you want me to do today?"

Judd just points to the sledgehammer again and doubles over laughin', like it's the biggest joke he ever played on somebody in his life. I can feel the sweat trickle down my back and I ain't even started yet.

Four o'clock comes, and I finally finished all that wood, but Judd pretends he's asleep. Got his head laid back, mouth half open, but I know it's just another way he's got to trick me. Wants me to sneak on home; then he'll say I never kept to my part of the bargain. So I go in his shed, put the sledgehammer back, take out the sickle, and go tackle the weeds down by his mailbox. Work on them weeds a whole hour, and when five o'clock comes, I start back toward the shed. See him watching me. I walk over.

"Sickle's gettin' dull, Judd. You got a whetstone around, I could sharpen it for you."

He studies me a good long while. "In the shed," he says.

I go get it, sit out on a stump, running the whetstone over the blade.

"Past five o'clock," says Judd.

"I know," I say.

"I ain't going to pay you one cent more," he says.

"It's okay," I tell him. Never saw look on a man's face like I see on his. Pure puzzlement is what it is.

Thing I decide on when I head for Judd's again the next day is that I got no choice. All I can do stick to my side of the deal and see what happens. All in the world I can do. If I quit now, he'll come for Shiloh, and we're right back where we started. I don't want to make him mad. No use having a winner and loser, or the bad feelings would just go on. Don't want to have to worry about Shiloh when he's running loose and I'm in school. Don't want to feel that Judd's so sore at me he'll think up any excuse at all to run his truck over my dog.

Only sign in this world we're making progress is the water Judd puts out for me. This day it even has ice in it, and Judd don't say one more word about a witness. In fact, when I'm through working and sit down on his porch to finish the water, Judd talks a little more than usual. Only bond we got between us is dogs, but at least that's somethin'.

I decide to say something nice to Judd. Tell him how good-looking his dogs are. Givin' a compliment to Judd Travers is like filling a balloon with air. You can actually see his chest swell up.

"Forty, thirty, and forty-five," he says, when I tell about his dogs.

"Those are their names now?"

"What I paid for 'em," he says.

"If they had a little more meat on their bones, I figure they'd be the best-lookin' hounds in Tyler County," I tell him.

Judd sits there, turnin' his beer around in his hands, and says, "Maybe could use a bit more fat."

I nurse my water along a little, too. "When'd you first get interested in hunting?" I ask him. "Your pa take you out when you was little?"

Judd spits. Didn't know a man could drink beer and chew tobacco at the same time, but Judd does. "Once or twice," he says. "Only nice thing about my dad I remember."

It's the first time in my life I ever felt anything like sorry for Judd Travers. If you weighed it on a postal scale, would hardly move the needle at all, but I suppose there was a fraction of an ounce of sorry for him somewhere inside me. When I thought on all the things I'd done with my own dad and how Judd could only remember hunting, well, that was pretty pitiful for a lifetime.

Thursday, when I get there, Judd's meanness has got the best of him again, because I can see he's running out of work for me to do, just giving me work to make me sweat. Dig a ditch to dump his garbage in, he says. Hoe that cornfield again, scrub that porch, weed that bean patch. But close on to five o'clock, he seems to realize that I'm only going to be there one more time. I'd worked real hard that day. Did anything he asked and done it better than he asked me to.

"Well, one more day," Judd says when I sit down at last with my water and him with his beer. "What you going to with that dog once he's yours?"

"Just play," I tell him. "Love him."

We sit there side by side while the clouds change places, puff out, the wind blowin' 'em this way and that. I'm wondering how things would have turned out if it hadn't been for that deer. If I'd just knocked on Judd's front door two weeks ago and told him I wasn't giving Shiloh up, what would have happen then?

To tell the truth, I think Ma's right. Judd would have sold him to me by and by because of Shiloh's limp. Judd's the kind that don't like that in a dog, same as he don't want a dent or a scratch of any kind on his pickup truck. Makes him look bad, he thinks. His truck's got to be perfect, to make up for all the ways Judd's not.

The last day I work for Judd, he inspects every job I do, finds fault with the least little thing. Keeps pesterin' me, makin' me hang around, do my work over. When it's time to go, I say, "Well, I guess that's it then."

Judd don't answer. Just stands in the doorway of his trailer looking at me, and then I get the feeling he's going to tell me I can take that paper he signed and use it for kindling. Tell me I can call the game warden if I want, there's not a trace of that deer left. The two weeks of work I put in for him was just long enough for rain to wash away the blood, for the field grass to spring back up again where the deer was shot.

He still don't say anything, though, so I start off for home, chest tight.

"Just a minute," says Judd.

I stop. He goes back inside the trailer, me waiting there in the yard. What am I going to say, he tries that? What am I going to do?

And then Judd's back in the doorway again, and he's got something in his hand. Comes down the steps halfway.

"Here," he says, and it's a dog's collar—an old collar, but better than the one Shiloh's got now. "Might be a little big, but he'll grow into it."

I look at Judd and take the collar. I don't know how we done it, but somehow we learned to get along.

"Thanks a lot," I tell him.

"You got yourself a dog," he says, and goes inside again, don't even look back.

I get home that evening, and Ma's baked a chocolate layer cake to celebrate—a real cake, too, not no Betty Crocker.

After dinner, Ma and Dad on the porch, the four of us rolls around on the grass together—Dara Lynn, Becky, Shiloh, and me. Becky tries to give Shiloh her butterfly kiss, but he don't hold still long enough to feel her eyelashes bat against him, just got to lick everywhere on her face.

And long after Becky and Dara Lynn goes inside, I lay out there on my back in the grass, not caring about the dew, Shiloh's against me crosswise, his paws on my chest.

I look at the dark closing in, sky getting more and more purple, and I'm thinking how nothing is as simple as you guess—not right or wrong, not Judd Travers, not even me or this dog I got here. But the good part is I saved Shiloh and opened my eyes some. Now that ain't bad for eleven.

Related Readings

Lois Lenski

The Christmas Fake

Having just enough money to get by does not keep this family from sharing their love.

THE RIDLEYS' HOUSE STOOD all alone back in the great piney woods. From the blacktop highway, a shady road wandered in and out around pine trees and palmettos to get to it. Sometimes trucks and wagons got stuck in the loose sand and had to be jacked up before they could be pulled out.

Two old live oak trees stood near the house, with broken branches and streams of Spanish moss hanging. The unpainted house, built of vertical battens,[1] had turned a dull gray from the ravages[2] of wind and weather. It had a porch across the front and four rooms inside. Under the house, several wild hogs were rooting.[3] Tangled, torn curtains hung at the windows and the front door stood wide open. Blocking the entrance lay three hound dogs outstretched. Their names were Trixie, Patches, and Jerry. Daddy insisted they were good watchdogs, but Mom said they were lazy and good-for-nothing.

Letty was ten, the oldest; Mike, seven; and little Punky, three. Besides Mom and Dad, there was Mom's sister, Aunt Vi, who spent most of her spare time with them. Mom didn't like living out in the backwoods so far from town, but the owner let them rent the house for almost nothing, so she tried to make the best of it.

---

1. **battens** sawed strips of wood
2. **ravages** devestating damage
3. **rooting** digging, as with a snout

The days were still as hot as midsummer. The only way anyone could tell that winter was coming was by the shortness of daylight. The sun seemed to set earlier every night. Just as soon as the big red ball slid down into the horizon, the dark dropped down like a heavy black curtain. The short days meant December, and December meant only one thing to the children. Christmas came to them in hot weather, not in cold. Christmas was green to them, never white. Having lived all their lives in the sunny South, they had never seen snow.

"How many days till Christmas?" asked Mike.

Letty, his sister, answered. First it was ten, then only seven, and now it was only one. Christmas was tomorrow.

"I want a doll and a buggy to ride her in," said little Punky.

"I want a bicycle and a BB gun and a football," said Mike.

"Forget it!" said Letty. "You won't get 'em."

"How do you know?" asked Mike.

"I asked Mom," said Letty. "She said there's no money for presents. I asked her if we could have a tree, and she said no money for a tree, either."

"I'll ask Santa Claus," said Mike.

Letty stared at her brother. Mike was seven now. Did he still believe in Santa Claus?

"Mom said she's gonna take us to town to see Santa Claus," Mike went on. "He's coming in a helicopter, landing right in City Park. I'll ask him for what I want."

Letty felt sad. She hated to tell Mike the truth. Let him believe in Santa as long as he could.

"Don't you remember when the man came and took our TV away?" she began. "'Cause Daddy only made the first payment?"

"Yes, and I fought him," said Mike. "Then he told us we could have it back after . . . Daddy got a job."

"Daddy got a job," said Letty, "but it's way over on the east coast. He can't even get home for Christmas. We never got the TV back, either. Don't you know that, Mike?"

"Yes, but we will," said Mike. "Daddy told me so, the last time he was home."

"He's got a job, but still there's no money for anything," said Letty bitterly.

"I know that," said Mike. "So I'll just ask Santa Claus . . ."

It was hopeless, so Letty said no more.

Mom said they could all go to town that afternoon to see Santa Claus. She made them wash their faces and necks and ears and arms and put their feet in the tin tub to get them clean. She got out clean clothes for them and they put shoes and stockings on. Letty's dress was patched, but it held together.

The Ridleys did not have a car. Daddy drove to his new job on the east coast with a neighbor who worked there, too. They left early Monday morning and did not return till late Saturday.

It was only a mile to town, not too far, except when Punky went along and got tired and had to be carried. Today Aunt Vi came by in her Ford and picked Mom and the children up. Aunt Vi had a job in an office in town. She typed letters for a real-estate man. She was having a few days off for Christmas.

When they got to town, Mom went with Aunt Vi to the beauty shop. Aunt Vi was to get a permanent, and Mom had to go to the supermarket for food. The children jumped out at Main Street. "Meet me at the bench at the corner," said Mom, "after Santa Claus leaves." It was too early for Santa Claus now, so Letty took Punky in the dime store. Mike saw some boys and went off with them.

How festive the little town looked! The light posts along the street were trimmed with tinsel and red paper bells. All the stores had Christmas decorations in their windows. From several, loudspeakers were blaring Christmas music. There were many shoppers going in and out. Everybody was happy because Christmas was coming.

Letty started down Main Street, pulling Punky by the hand. Punky broke loose and dashed on ahead. So Letty had to skip along fast to keep up. Inside the store, Punky ran down the aisle and picked things off the counters. Letty made her put them back and slapped her hands.

Letty had two dollars of her own in her pocket. She had earned it baby-sitting for the Boyers. They had four little ones under six and she often sat with them. She went to the jewelry counter. She wanted a pretty brass pin to wear on her shoulder. There were so many it was hard to choose. They were only twenty-five cents. If there wasn't going to be any Christmas at home, at least she could buy herself a present. She'd still have $1.75 left to help pay for that new coat she needed.

"Is that your little sister?" asked the clerk.

Letty heard a child crying but did not look up.

"Yes," she said. "She bothers the daylights out of me. Keeps me runnin' my legs off. I get mad at her. I take her by the arm and jerk her."

"Better watch her now," said the clerk. "She's helping herself to a doll. Guess she's too little to know you have to pay for things in here."

"Do you know what I do to make her mind?" asked Letty.

"No," said the clerk, "but you'd better do it quick."

"I spank her," said Letty. "Not when my mother's around, of course. I spank her with my hand—hard, too!"

She rushed over to Punky, took the doll out of her hand, and spanked her. Punky screamed and stamped her foot.

"Now you keep still," said Letty, "or I'll take you home."

Letty dragged her back to the jewelry counter.

"Does spanking make her better?" asked the clerk.

"Well, no," said Letty. "The more I spank her, the more I have to spank her."

Punky ran back to the doll counter. She picked up the doll again.

"She really wants that doll," said the clerk.

"Oh, she wants everything she sees," said Letty. "She's always saying 'gimme, gimme. . . .'"

Punky called out: "I want it, Letty, I want it. . . ."

"Well, you can't have it!" answered Letty. She bent over the jewelry counter again. Should she get the flying bird or the butterfly? The brooches[4] were all so pretty, she could not decide which one she liked best.

"Has she got a doll at home?" asked the clerk.

"No," said Letty. "She's had dozens, but she breaks 'em all up."

"She ought to have one," said the clerk. "Why don't you buy that doll for her? Then maybe you could keep her quiet. A little girl like that needs a doll to love and play with."

Letty looked up, startled. What business was it of the clerk's? She opened her purse. In that moment, she had an important decision to make. She looked across to the toy counter, where Punky was holding up the doll. It was just a cheap one. She saw its price tag—49¢. Then she looked down at the butterfly brooch in her hand.

---

4. **brooches** large ornamental pins

"I'll take this," she said. She handed the clerk a quarter.

The clerk made no comment. She put the brooch in a small paper bag and rang up the money.

Letty rushed over and jerked Punky away from the toy counter. Punky began to cry. "I want a dolly. . . . I want my mama. . . . I wanna go home. . . ."

The clerk came over and spoke again: "Do you ever read her a story? Or take her for a ride in her little wagon?"

"What wagon?" Letty stared at the clerk. "Punky hasn't got any little wagon."

"She'd be a pretty little girl," said the clerk, "if you'd wash her face."

"She bothers the daylights out of me," said Letty.

Out on the sidewalk, Punky was still crying. Letty leaned over and wiped her tears away.

"Do you want to see Santa Claus?" Letty asked.

"Yes," said Punky.

"We'll go see Santa Claus, and you can ask him for a dolly," said Letty. "Tell him you want a great big doll as big as a baby. . . ."

Punky smiled. "As big as a baby," she said.

The little City Park was crowded now, with children of all sizes and ages. Men from the Jaycees[5] were herding them into a long line.

"Get in line! Take your turn!" the men shouted.

Overhead, a loud buzzing sound could be heard. The children's eyes all turned toward the sky. There, coming closer and closer, was a helicopter. It slowed up, then came straight down in a roped-off open spot. The door opened and Santa Claus stepped out. He was very fat, dressed in a bright red suit, and he had a white mustache and a long white beard. The children screamed with delight.

Letty looked over the crowd and finally spotted Mike. She called to him. Mike made his way over to her and they waited their turn, holding Punky tightly by the hands. Once Letty lifted Punky up so she could see Santa Claus.

The children in the line asked for everything under the sun from bicycles, typewriters, and pianos to parakeets, rabbits, and turtles. The line moved slowly toward the big fat Santa Claus.

---

5. **Jaycees** Junior Chamber of Commerce, a community organization of young businesspeople

"We're next!" said Letty, pushing Mike forward.

Mike never forgot for a minute.

"I want a bicycle, a BB gun, and a football," he said in a loud voice.

Santa patted him on the back.

"I'll do what I can for you, son," he said and shoved him along. "Who's next?"

Now it was Punky's turn. She stared at the big fat man and his white whiskers, half frightened.

Letty leaned over. "Say what you want, Punky," she prompted.[6] "Tell him you want a buggy and a doll. . . ."

"I want . . ." began Punky. "I want *a great big doll as big as a baby!*"

Santa laughed. "You be a good girl, now," he said, "and I'll try to get it for you, honey."

Then he turned to Letty.

"You're too old . . ." he began.

"I want a watch!" said Letty emphatically.[7] "Not a Mickey Mouse one—I'm too big for that. A real one, I want this time. That's the only thing I want. I don't care if I get candy or anything else—just a wristwatch!"

Santa eyed her coldly.

"What if you don't get it?" he said.

Letty shrugged. "I'll be satisfied with what I get, even if it's nothing. That's all I can do, I reckon."

But Santa was not listening. He had shoved her quickly aside. He was beaming and smiling and making rash[8] promises to all the children coming behind.

When they got out of the crowd, Letty said to Mike, "Oh, I hate that guy!"

"Who?" said Mike.

"That fool of a Santa Claus," said Letty.

Mike's eyes opened wide.

"Why, he's going to bring us"—Mike began—"the things we asked for!"

---

6. **prompted** reminded; encouraged

7. **emphatically** forcefully

8. **rash** reckless; irresponsible

"Oh, no, he's not!" cried Letty angrily. "He's tellin' lies—to all the kids in town, makin' them believe he'll bring them anything they ask for!"

Mike's face turned white. "You mean . . . ?"

Punky began to cry.

Letty did not stop there.

"Santa Claus is just a fake—a big Christmas *fake*!" she said. "I don't believe anything like that. Three years ago I knew it. I got up that Christmas Eve night to see Santa, and it wasn't him. It was Grandma. I saw her—not even Daddy—puttin' presents out."

The sparkle in Mike's eyes faded as they filled with tears.

Then suddenly Mom and Aunt Vi came up and Aunt Vi told them where the car was parked.

"Did you tell Santa what you want?" asked Aunt Vi.

"Yes," said Punky. "He said he's gonna bring me a dolly."

"I asked for a bike," said Mike, soberly, "but he don't have to bring it if he don't want to."

Letty lagged behind.

She looked around sharply. Mom and Aunt Vi had no packages under their arms and she saw none in Aunt Vi's car. They had gone shopping but had bought nothing. Santa Claus was just a fake, and so was Christmas. Now she was sure of it.

"I'm gonna walk home," she told Mom.

"Okay," said Mom. "Better get there by supper time if you want anything to eat."

Letty walked slowly home, with a heavy heart. She hated the decorations on the street now and the sound of the Christmas music. What good was it all? There would be no Christmas at home. Mom had told her so. The only promise Mom made was, if Dad got the day off, they might eat out and go to a show. Whenever they ate out, Letty took two hot dogs and ice cream. What fun was that?

Letty came to a vacant lot where Christmas trees were being sold. A young man came rushing out and tried to urge her to buy a tree.

What good was a Christmas tree?

Then Letty stopped in her tracks. Maybe . . . maybe they could have a tree, at least. It would be better than no Christmas at all. There was a box of shiny balls and a string of electric lights left over from a couple of years before. She knew just where they were, on the bottom shelf of the kitchen cupboard.

Why not have a tree . . . with lights on it?

It would be better than nothing. Especially if there were no presents. Punky would like the pretty lights if she couldn't have a doll-baby.

But the trees were not cheap.

"Two dollars each," said the man, holding one up.

"It's too big," said Letty. "Have you got a smaller one?"

The man found a smaller one, but it was two dollars, too.

Letty looked in her purse. All she had left was $1.75. If only she hadn't bought the brooch.

"You got a car?" asked the man. "Where'll I take it?"

"I'm walking," said Letty. "I'll carry it."

The man laughed as if it was a big joke.

"Carry it?" he cried. "A skinny little kid like you?"

Now he was more friendly.

"I'll tell you what I'll do," he said. He found a nice tree for her. "This one's a little lopsided, but you can have it for one-fifty. That'll leave you twenty-five cents for a taxi. Here's a taxi now."

A man got out of the taxi and Letty got in with her tree. The man called, "Merry Christmas!" after her. The taxi driver took her and the tree home for twenty-five cents.

It was nearly dark when she got there. Days were short now in December, and night clamped down early. The three dogs were on the porch as usual, Trixie, Patches, and Jerry. They slept on the porch to keep burglars away.

Now they thought Letty was a burglar. They barked and barked as she came up, pulling the tree behind her. Now everybody would see it. Letty had hoped supper would be over and Punky and Mike in bed and, of course, Dad not home yet. Dad was not coming home for Christmas! She wanted to set the tree up in the front room and surprise them all.

But they were all there eating supper—Aunt Vi, too; of course, not Dad. Punky had fallen asleep on the couch. Mom called to Letty but Letty was too excited now to eat supper. She put up the tree all by herself. She found Dad's hammer and fixed a brace at the bottom to keep it from falling over. She found the lights and the cord and put them on. She tied the shiny balls on. She turned the switch and the tree looked beautiful.

Then Punky woke up. How surprised she was to see a tree with lights on it! On Christmas Eve, too!

Punky danced around the tree and tripped over the light cord. She grabbed the cord and pulled it. The lights went out. Punky pulled the colored balls off. She dropped one of them and broke it.

Letty took Punky and spanked her.

She plugged the cord in again and put the balls back on.

At least it was something for Christmas.

Letty was tired now and felt like going to bed. She reached for a hot dog off the table and gulped it down. It was all she wanted to eat. She wasn't hungry.

She and Mike looked at each other. They looked round the house. There were no signs of Christmas—except the tree.

"I paid all my baby-sitting money for it!" Letty bragged.

Mom scolded. "You were saving for a new coat. You need a coat more than we need a tree."

Letty turned to Mike. "Tomorrow's Christmas. No presents anywhere. Didn't I tell you?" she whispered.

It was in the middle of the night when Daddy came and wakened them. That is, it seemed like the middle of the night. It was really six in the morning.

"Merry Christmas! Merry Christmas!" shouted Daddy. When did he come? How did he get there? Did he get an unexpected day off?

Dad was wheeling a bike. Where had it come from?

"But, Mom!" cried Letty. She rubbed her eyes as if she'd been dreaming. "You said there was no money. . . ."

Mike was so happy, he did not ask where the bike came from. He did not notice that it was scuffed and secondhand. It was a bike at last.

Mom was opening a big box beside her. She took a small one out and handed it to Letty. Letty opened it. There lay a wristwatch—a real one, not a Mickey Mouse one. Letty could not believe her eyes.

"So you won't miss the school bus," said Mom.

Letty threw her arms around Mom's neck. Then she hugged Dad.

"You are both *fakes!*" she cried. "Mom said there was no money . . . and that Dad couldn't get home. . . ."

Best of all was Punky's doll. It had blue eyes that closed, yellow curls, and white teeth. It was as big as a baby, as big as Punky could hold. She walked up and down, patting the doll and singing to it.

Letty plugged in the lights on the tree. Dad stared. "Where on earth did *that* come from?"

Letty still could not understand. She looked from Mom to Dad. How did they find out about the bike and the watch and the doll? She forgot that she and Mike and Punky had been talking about what they wanted for weeks in advance.

Mike had the answer.

"Santa Claus brought them," he said.

Suddenly Letty thought of something. She ran into the bedroom and came out with a little box. She took out the beautiful butterfly brooch. She had wanted it for herself, but now it was Christmas, so she knew what she wanted to do. She'd give it to Mom.

She turned to Mom and pinned it on her shoulder.

"Merry Christmas, Mom!" she said.

"What! For *me?*" cried Mom.

Mom kissed her and they all said, "Merry Christmas!"

from
Stride Toward Freedom

Martin Luther King Jr.

In 1955, African American citizens in Montgomery, Alabama, united to challenge a law that segregated them from white citizens. The city of Montgomery had a law that forbade African American people from riding in the front of a bus. If a white person boarded the bus, a black person was supposed to give up a seat and move farther to the rear of the bus. On December 1, 1955, Rosa Parks was sitting in the first row of seats in the black section of the bus. When the bus driver ordered her to move to the back because some white men had gotten on, Parks refused. The bus driver called the police to have her arrested.

The leaders in the African American community in Montgomery immediately planned a large scale boycott of Montgomery city buses. Dr. Martin Luther King Jr., who was the pastor at the Baptist church in Montgomery, called for a meeting to plan the boycott, which began on December 5, 1955. Almost a year later, in November 1956, the Supreme Court declared that segregation on public buses is unconstitutional. The bus integration order reached Montgomery on December 20. A mass meeting was scheduled to give the people instructions before returning to the buses the following day. This passage starts with King's description of the close of that mass meeting.

AT THE CLOSE OF THE MEETING I asked the ministers to stay over for a few minutes to urge them to ride the buses during the rush hours for the first few days. It was our feeling that their presence would give the Negro citizens courage and make them less likely to retaliate[1] in case of insults. The ministers readily agreed. Accordingly, two were assigned to each bus line in the city, to ride mainly during the morning and afternoon rush. They were given suggestions as to how to handle situations of violence and urged to keep an accurate record of all incidents.

I had decided that after many months of struggling with my people for the goal of justice I should not sit back and watch, but should lead them back to the buses myself. I asked Ralph Abernathy, E. D. Nixon, and Glenn Smiley to join me in riding on the first integrated[2] bus. They reached my house around 5:45 on Friday morning. Television cameras, photographers, and news reporters were hovering outside the door. At 5:55 we walked toward the bus stop, the cameras shooting, the reporters bombarding[3] us with questions. Soon the bus appeared; the door opened, and I stepped on. The bus driver greeted me with a cordial[4] smile. As I put my fare in the box he said:

"I believe you are Reverend King, aren't you?"

I answered: "Yes I am."

"We are glad to have you this morning," he said.

I thanked him and took my seat, smiling now too. Abernathy, Nixon, and Smiley followed, with several reporters and television men behind them. Glenn Smiley sat next to me. So I rode the first integrated bus in Montgomery with a white minister, and a native southerner, as my seatmate.

Downtown we transferred to one of the buses that serviced the white residential section. As the white people boarded, many took seats as if nothing were going on. Others looked amazed to see Negroes sitting in front, and some appeared peeved to know that they either had to sit behind Negroes or stand. One elderly man stood up by the conductor, despite the fact that there were several vacant seats

---

1. **retaliate** fight back
2. **integrated** open to people of all races or ethnic groups, without restriction
3. **bombarding** attacking persistently
4. **cordial** warm and friendly

in the rear. When someone suggested to him that he sit in back, he responded: "I would rather die and go to hell than sit behind a nigger." A white woman unknowingly took a seat by a Negro. When she noticed her neighbor, she jumped up and said in a tone of obvious anger: "What are these niggers gonna do next?"

But despite such signs of hostility[5] there were no major incidents on the first day. Many of the whites responded to the new system calmly. Several deliberately and with friendly smiles took seats beside Negroes. True, one Negro woman was slapped by a white man as she alighted,[6] but she refused to retaliate. Later she said: "I could have broken that little fellow's neck all by myself, but I left the mass meeting last night determined to do what Reverend King asked." The *Montgomery Advertiser* reported at the end of the first day: "The calm but cautious acceptance of this significant change in Montgomery's way of life came without any major disturbance."

But the reactionaries[7] were not in retreat. Many of them had predicted violence, and such predictions are always a conscious or unconscious invitation to action. When people, especially in public office, talk about bloodshed as a concomitant[8] of integration, they stir and arouse the hoodlums[9] to acts of destruction, and often work under cover to bring them about. In Montgomery several public officials had predicted violence, and violence there had to be if they were to save face.

By December 28 the first few days of peaceful compliance[10] had given way to a reign of terror.[11] City buses were fired on throughout the city, especially in poorly lighted sections. A teenage girl was beaten by four or five white men as she alighted from a bus. A pregnant Negro woman was shot in the leg. Fearfully, many Negroes and whites refused to ride the buses. The city commission responded by suspending the night runs on city lines. No bus could begin a run after

---

5. **hostility** anger and ill will, as among enemies
6. **alighted** stepped down
7. **reactionaries** those who are opposed to change
8. **concomitant** accompaniment
9. **hoodlums** rough, brutal, violent people
10. **compliance** acting according to the law
11. **reign of terror** period of time marked by violence

five o'clock, which meant that once again returning workers were without transportation. This was exactly what the violent elements wanted.

During this period a new effort was made to divide the Negroes. Handbills[12] were distributed urging Negroes to rebel against me in particular and their leaders in general. These leaflets purported to come from "fed-up" Negroes, but virtually everyone knew that they were the work of white extremists.[13] Referring to me as Luther, one leaflet said: "We get shot at while he rides. He is getting us in more trouble every day. Wake up. Run him out of town." Another one stated: "We have been doing OK in Montgomery before outside preachers were born! Ask Reverend King's papa & mamma if they like his doings—ask him if they going to help in Atlanta. Better quit him before it is too late!"

The KKK[14] was in its element. One day it descended upon Montgomery in full regalia.[15] But it seemed to have lost its spell. A college student who saw the Klansmen swarming the streets in their white costumes with red insignia[16] went cheerfully on about her business, thinking that they were collecting for the United Fund. And one cold night a small Negro boy was seen warming his hands at a burning cross.

On January 9, Ralph Abernathy and I went to Atlanta to prepare for a meeting of Negro leaders that I had called for the following day. In the middle of the night we were awakened by a telephone call from Ralph's wife, Juanita. I knew that only some new disaster would make her rouse us at two in the morning. When Ralph came back, his sober face told part of the story. "My home has been bombed," he said, "and three or four other explosions have been heard in the city, but Juanita doesn't know where yet." I asked about Juanita and their daughter. "Thank God, they are safe." Before we could talk any more, the telephone rang a second time. It was Juanita again, saying that the First Baptist Church had been hit. I looked at Ralph as he sat down beside me, stunned. Both his home and his church bombed in one night,

---

12. **handbills** announcements or advertisements distributed by hand
13. **extremists** people wanting to take drastic measures or holding severe viewpoints
14. **KKK** Ku Klux Klan
15. **regalia** distinguishing dress
16. **insignia** emblem, badge, or other distinguishing mark

and I knew no words to comfort him. There in the early morning hours we prayed to God together, asking for the power of endurance,[17] the strength to carry on.

Between three and seven we received no less than fifteen calls. We finally learned that besides Ralph's home and church, Bob Graetz's home and three other Baptist churches—Bell Street, Hutchinson Street, and Mt. Olive—had all been hit. Worrying that this time the people might be goaded[18] into striking back, I called a few ministers in Montgomery and urged them to do what they could to keep control. In the meantime, Ralph and I arranged to fly back, leaving the meeting of southern leaders to begin without us.

From the Montgomery airport we drove directly to Ralph's house. The street was roped off, and hundreds of people stood staring at the ruins. The front porch had been almost completely destroyed, and things inside the house were scattered from top to bottom. Juanita, though shocked and pale, was fairly composed.

The rest of the morning was spent in a grim tour of the other bombings. The Bell Street and Mt. Olive Baptist churches had been almost completely destroyed. The other two churches were less severely damaged, but nevertheless faced great losses. The total damage to the four churches was estimated at $70,000. Bob Graetz's home had been a bomb target the previous summer, but had escaped serious damage. This time he was not so fortunate. The front of his house lay in ruins, and shattered glass throughout the interior showed the violence of the explosion. Assembled at each of the bombed sites was a large group of angry people; but with a restraint[19] that I never ceased to wonder at, they held themselves under control.

The next morning, three important white agencies issued statements condemning the bombings. Grover Hall, editor of the *Montgomery Advertiser,* wrote a strong editorial entitled "Is it safe to live in Montgomery?" in which he insisted that the issue had gone beyond the question of segregation versus integration. As I read Hall's strong statement I could not help admiring this brilliant but complex man who claimed to be a supporter of segregation but could not stomach the excesses performed in its name. Several white ministers

---

17. **endurance**   ability to bear up under hardships
18. **goaded**   urged; driven
19. **restraint**   holding back; reserve

denounced the bombing as unchristian and uncivilized, and all through the day their statement was repeated over television by the distinguished minister of the First Presbyterian Church, Rev. Merle Patterson. The Men of Montgomery, too, made known their unalterable opposition to the bombings. For the first time since the protest began, these influential whites were on public record on the side of law and order. Their stands gave us new confidence in the basic decency of the vast majority of whites in the community. Despite their commitment to segregation, it was clear that they were still law-abiding, and would never sanction[20] the use of violence to preserve the system.

That afternoon, I returned to Atlanta to make at least an appearance at the meeting of Negro leaders. There I found an enthusiastic group of almost a hundred men from all over the South, committed to the idea of a southern movement to implement the Supreme Court's decision against bus segregation through nonviolent means. Before adjourning[21] they voted to form a permanent organization, the Southern Christian Leadership Conference, and elected me president, a position I still hold.

When I returned to Montgomery over the weekend I found the Negro community in low spirits. After the bombings the city commission had ordered all buses off the streets; and it now appeared that the city fathers would use this reign of violence as an excuse to cancel the bus company's franchise.[22] As a result, many were coming to feel that all our gains had been lost; and I myself started to fear that we were in for another long struggle to get bus service renewed. I was also beginning to wonder whether the virulent[23] leaflets that were bombarding the Negro community might be having their effect. Discouraged, and still revolted by the bombings, for some strange reason I began to feel a personal sense of guilt for everything that was happening.

In this mood I went to the mass meeting on Monday night. There for the first time, I broke down in public. I had invited the audience to join me in prayer, and had begun by asking God's guidance and

---

20. **sanction** give approval, support, or encouragement to
21. **adjourning** stopping work or proceedings
22. **franchise** charter; right to operate
23. **virulent** harmful; full of hate and bitterness

direction in all our activities. Then, in the grip of an emotion I could not control, I said, "Lord, I hope no one will have to die as a result of our struggle for freedom in Montgomery. Certainly I don't want to die. But if anyone has to die, let it be me." The audience was in an uproar. Shouts and cries of "no, no" came from all sides. So intense was the reaction, that I could not go on with my prayer. Two of my fellow ministers came to the pulpit[24] and suggested that I take a seat. For a few minutes I stood with their arms around me, unable to move. Finally, with the help of my friends, I sat down. It was this scene that caused the press to report mistakenly that I had collapsed.

Unexpectedly, this episode brought me great relief. Many people came up to me after the meeting and many called the following day to assure me that we were all together until the end. For the next few days, the city was fairly quiet. Bus service was soon resumed, though still on a daytime schedule only.

Then another wave of terror hit. Early in the morning of January 28, the People's Service Station and Cab Stand was bombed, and another bomb fell at the home of Allen Robertson, a sixty-year-old Negro hospital worker. It was never discovered why these two victims had been singled out for attack. The same morning an unexploded bomb, crudely[25] assembled from twelve sticks of dynamite, was found still smoldering[26] on my porch.

I was staying with friends on the other side of town, and Coretta and "Yoki" were in Atlanta. So once more I heard the news first on the telephone. On my way home, I visited the other scenes of disaster nearby, and found to my relief that no one had been hurt. I noticed a police car driving away from the area with two Negroes on the rear seat. These men, I learned, were under arrest because they had challenged the police to their faces with having done nothing to catch the bombers. Both were later convicted of trying to "incite[27] to riot." But there was no riot that day, although the crowds that had gathered around the damaged buildings were once again ready for violence. They were just waiting for a signal. Fortunately, the signal never came.

At home I addressed the crowd from my porch, where the mark of

---

24. **pulpit** raised structure from which a minister delivers a sermon or conducts a worship service
25. **crudely** roughly; shoddily
26. **smoldering** burning and smoking with little or no flame
27. **incite** urge; rouse

the bomb was clear. "We must not return violence under any condition. I know this is difficult advice to follow, especially since we have been the victims of no less than ten bombings. But this is the way of Christ; it is the way of the cross. We must somehow believe that unearned suffering is redemptive."[28] Then since it was Sunday morning, I urged the people to go home and get ready for church. Gradually they dispersed.[29]

---

28. **redemptive** bringing about recovery from harm or distress
29. **dispersed** scattered; broke up and went in different directions

Ezra Bowen

What Ever Became of Honest Abe?

Are people today more dishonest than in the past? Are there some situations in which dishonesty is acceptable? This 1988 magazine article indicates that not everyone struggles over breaking the law.

THE MONEY IS SITTING THERE for the taking, in a lost wallet or valise,[1] in an open armored car, or just blowing around in untraceable bills. And no cops in sight. Do you snatch the cash and run? Or do you turn it in? Or try to find the owner?

Such moral[2] questions, involving what might be called target-of-opportunity theft, come up more often than most people suspect. When bags of cash tumbled from an armored truck . . . in Columbus, . . . in San Francisco and again . . . in Toronto, most of the money was grabbed by passersby. Of the $765,000 lost in San Francisco, some $400,000 is still missing. Two men returned much of the balance to Loomis Armored Inc. The next day an anonymous woman, worn down by a guilty conscience, gave back $28,000.

But many consciences do not seem quite so bothered when they can make a quick buck without committing robbery or burglary. Says Philosophy Professor John Hospers of the University of Southern California: "There are people who feel that they have been had by society, so if they can get back at society by taking whatever they find in the street, it's strictly retaliation."[3] It is also strictly illegal, though

---

1. **valise** piece of hand luggage, often a type of large briefcase
2. **moral** relating to the difference between right and wrong in behavior
3. **retaliation** payback for an injury or wrong

most people are not aware of that until after they make their grab. Loomis has had calls from four men offering to give back the cash in return for rewards, plus immunity from California's felony[4] law against finders-keepers, which applies to amounts above $400.

The Ohio episode proved to be a mass test of reaction to unexpected riches. Dozens of motorists scooped up an estimated $2 million in bulging moneybags and bills fluttering in the wind; perhaps $100,000 came back. And when Melvin Kiser, an Ohio Bell repairman, voluntarily returned $57,000, approval of his deed was not uniform. "My mother said she was proud of me," reports Kiser, "that that's the way she raised me. But my dad said, 'I thought I raised you better than that.'"

Honest Mel and a few others clearly are throwbacks.[5] Nowadays Abraham Lincoln would apparently be trudging pretty much alone on his high-minded mission to return that 6¼¢ in change that a customer inadvertently[6] overpaid. Phone-in listeners to Columbus radio station WTVN indicated that some 60% would have taken the money on the freeway. Concern about a general ethical decline has so troubled Columbus Mayor Dana Rinehart that he formed a commission on ethics[7] and values, headed by none other than (are you ready, America?) Jeb Stuart Magruder.

Magruder, a Watergate ex-con reconstituted[8] as a Presbyterian minister, sees himself well qualified for the role. He became interested, he says, "because I had been involved in one of the great scandals of this country." Adds Magruder: "Not only do people seem to be willing to take money off the streets, but our leaders seem to be doing the same thing. If you have leaders who have that kind of ethical standard, there's no reason to expect the rest of the people" to do better.

High rank or low, "it is rare for people to think that they have straight out done something wrong," observes Judith Lichtenberg of the Institute for Philosophy and Public Policy at the University of Maryland. So they take refuge in rationales.[9] Says Columbia

---

4. **felony** major crime, usually punished by imprisonment
5. **throwbacks** examples of earlier beliefs
6. **inadvertently** unintentionally; accidently
7. **ethics** standards of right and wrong
8. **reconstituted** remade
9. **rationales** explanations of reasons

University's Thomas Pogge, an assistant professor of philosophy: "The first distinction[10] many make is whether or not you are directly stealing from an individual. If so, it is more immoral. The second distinction is whether or not the victim is poor. If poor, the stealing is worse." Least objectionable to most people, both Pogge and Lichtenberg agree, is stealing from the government or an institution. Abstractly[11] there may be no moral difference, but in practice, many apparently agree with a coworker of Honest Mel's who said in disbelief, "That was a gift from God and you gave it back."

---

10. **distinction** difference
11. **abstractly** in thought, idea, or belief

Cynthia Rylant | # Stray

Doris unexpectedly finds an animal to love. But can her family afford to keep it?

In January, a puppy wandered onto the property of Mr. Amos Lacey and his wife, Mamie, and their daughter, Doris. Icicles hung three feet or more from the eaves of houses, snowdrifts swallowed up automobiles and the birds were so fluffed up they looked comic.

The puppy had been abandoned, and it made its way down the road toward the Laceys' small house, its ears tucked, its tail between its legs, shivering.

Doris, whose school had been called off because of the snow, was out shoveling the cinderblock front steps when she spotted the pup on the road. She set down the shovel.

"Hey! Come on!" she called.

The puppy stopped in the road, wagging its tail timidly, trembling with shyness and cold.

Doris trudged through the yard, went up the shoveled drive and met the dog.

"Come on, Pooch."

"Where did *that* come from?" Mrs. Lacey asked as soon as Doris put the dog down in the kitchen.

Mr. Lacey was at the table, cleaning his fingernails with his pocketknife. The snow was keeping him home from his job at the warehouse.

"I don't know where it came from," he said mildly, "but I know for sure where it's going."

Doris hugged the puppy hard against her. She said nothing.

Because the roads would be too bad for travel for many days, Mr. Lacey couldn't get out to take the puppy to the pound in the city right away. He agreed to let it sleep in the basement while Mrs. Lacey grudgingly[1] let Doris feed it table scraps. The woman was sensitive about throwing out food.

By the looks of it, Doris figured the puppy was about six months old, and on its way to being a big dog. She thought it might have some shepherd in it.

Four days passed and the puppy did not complain. It never cried in the night or howled at the wind. It didn't tear up everything in the basement. It wouldn't even follow Doris up the basement steps unless it was invited.

It was a good dog.

Several times Doris had opened the door in the kitchen that led to the basement and the puppy had been there, all stretched out, on the top step. Doris knew it had wanted some company and that it had lain against the door, listening to the talk in the kitchen, smelling the food, being a part of things. It always wagged its tail, eyes all sleepy, when she found it there.

Even after a week had gone by, Doris didn't name the dog. She knew her parents wouldn't let her keep it, that her father made so little money any pets were out of the question, and that the pup would definitely go to the pound when the weather cleared.

Still, she tried talking to them about the dog at dinner one night.

"She's a good dog, isn't she?" Doris said, hoping one of them would agree with her.

Her parents glanced at each other and went on eating.

"She's not much trouble," Doris added. "I like her." She smiled at them, but they continued to ignore her.

"I figure she's real smart," Doris said to her mother. "I could teach her things."

Mrs. Lacey just shook her head and stuffed a forkful of sweet potato in her mouth. Doris fell silent, praying the weather would never clear.

But on Saturday, nine days after the dog had arrived, the sun was shining and the roads were plowed. Mr. Lacey opened up the trunk of his car and came into the house.

Doris was sitting alone in the living room, hugging a pillow and rocking back and forth on the edge of a chair. She was trying not to cry but she was not strong enough. Her face was wet and red, her eyes full of distress.

---

1. **grudgingly** reluctantly

Mrs. Lacey looked into the room from the doorway.

"Mama," Doris said in a small voice. "Please."

Mrs. Lacey shook her head.

"You know we can't afford a dog, Doris. You try to act more grown-up about this."

Doris pressed her face into the pillow.

Outside, she heard the trunk of the car slam shut, one of the doors open and close, the old engine cough and choke and finally start up.

"Daddy," she whispered. "Please."

She heard the car travel down the road, and, though it was early afternoon, she could do nothing but go to her bed. She cried herself to sleep, and her dreams were full of searching and searching for things lost.

It was nearly night when she finally woke up. Lying there, like stone, still exhausted, she wondered if she would ever in her life have anything. She stared at the wall for a while.

But she started feeling hungry, and she knew she'd have to make herself get out of bed and eat some dinner. She wanted not to go into the kitchen, past the basement door. She wanted not to face her parents.

But she rose up heavily.

Her parents were sitting at the table, dinner over, drinking coffee. They looked at her when she came in, but she kept her head down. No one spoke.

Doris made herself a glass of powdered milk and drank it all down. Then she picked up a cold biscuit and started out of the room.

"You'd better feed that mutt before it dies of starvation," Mr. Lacey said.

Doris turned around.

"What?"

"I said, you'd better feed your dog. I figure it's looking for you."

Doris put her hand to her mouth.

"You didn't take her?" she asked.

"Oh, I took her all right," her father answered. "Worst looking place I've ever seen. Ten dogs to a cage. Smell was enough to knock you down. And they give an animal six days to live. Then they kill it with some kind of a shot."

Doris stared at her father.

"I wouldn't leave an *ant* in that place," he said. "So I brought the dog back."

Mrs. Lacey was smiling at him and shaking her head as if she would never, ever, understand him.

Mr. Lacey sipped his coffee.

"Well," he said, "are you going to feed it or not?"

Italian folktale retold by Sharon Creeden

The Bell of Atri

Many countries besides the United States have laws to protect animals from mistreatment. This Italian folktale focuses on the abuse of an animal and its results. The folktale is followed by an overview of animal rights in the United States.

LONG AGO, THERE WAS A TOWN in Italy called Atri. Because the people desired harmony and justice, they hung a large bell in the center of the town. The people said, "Anyone who has been wronged can ring the bell. We will all gather and settle the dispute."

Years passed, and no one rang the bell. Perhaps just seeing the bell in the square caused the citizens to deal fairly with each other. The rope of the bell hung to the ground; over time, a grape vine twined around it.

During those years, a knight returned to Atri from foreign wars. He rode into town on his strong and beautiful horse. He told everyone of the battles. "The only reason I am alive is because this swift steed[1] carried me safely out of danger. I will be grateful all of her days," he told the people.

The knight returned to his farm and put away his sword and armor. He put his beloved horse in a warm stall. "I promise you, my brave friend, you will always have a bed and a bucket of oats." But the horse had been exhausted and chilled in the battles and began to decline in health. At first, the knight took tender care of his animal.

Slowly, the knight forgot about his battles; he became just a busy farmer tending his stock and tilling[2] the soil. The once brave and beautiful horse was now deaf and blind. "You eat too much and you

---

1. **steed** horse

take up too much space," the master said. Finally, one day, he said, "You are useless." He felt justified[3] in taking the old horse out of the stable, taking off her bridle, and driving her off with a stick.

The old horse was confused. She stood outside the gate with her head hung down. Night fell and the wind and snow came. The horse began to stumble around to find shelter and food. In her blind search, she walked toward town. By dawn, the horse was standing in the village square. She chanced upon the rope of the bell which hung to the ground. She began to nibble on the vine encircling the rope. The bell began to ring.

The people poured into the street. "Who calls for justice?" they asked. Everyone knew the knight's horse. The saw her; thin, blind and covered with snow. But they remembered her hour of glory when her master had promised gratitude. "She has a right to ring the bell and demand justice," the people agreed.

The knight was called before the town to explain his cruel behavior; he had no explanation. He was ordered to take care of his horse and treat her with loving kindness for all of her days. The faithful horse was led home to a warm stall and a bucket of oats.

$$* \quad * \quad * \quad * \quad * \quad *$$

Comments
Anti-cruelty Laws
The United States was the first country to enact laws to protect animals from cruel treatment. In 1641, the Puritans voted on their legal code, "The Body of Liberties," which contained one hundred liberties to be observed. Liberty 92 declared that cruelty to animals was forbidden: "No man shall exercise any Tirranny[4] or Crueltie towards any bruite Creature which are usuallie kept for man's use." Currently, all fifty states have anti-cruelty laws that generally say that animals have the right to:
- Food, water and shelter.
- Protection from cruel treatment.
- Protection from abandonment.
- Protection from poisoning.

---

2. **tilling** working to raise crops; plowing, fertilizing, and cultivating

3. **justified** right; blameless

4. **Tirranny (tyranny)** harshness; cruel or unjust use of power

Animal Protection Societies

Although there are laws to protect animals, as a nation, we abandon thousands of animals each year. As a result, there are groups that maintain shelters for unwanted animals and investigate reports of animal mistreatment. In 1866, the first anti-cruelty society was founded by Henry Bergh. The American Society for the Prevention of Cruelty to Animals (ASPCA) became the model for about one thousand local societies in the United States. For example, storyteller Pat Peterson is a member of the Cascade Animal Protection Society. She rescues abandoned cats, takes them for medical treatment, and gives them foster care until they are placed with a family. She is still fostering a handsome white cat, Buddy, who I found injured and hungry in the traffic in front of my condo in Seattle.

Animal Rights

Our national attitudes towards animals have changed significantly since the Pilgrims arrived and we began the expansion into the West. We no longer condone[5] the slaughter of bison and wildlife, for example. Animal rights debates remain, however, extremely divisive.[6] Common conflicting opinions include:

- Animals should not be used for experiments because it is inhumane,[7] inadequately regulated and is of no benefit **vs.** animal experimentation is necessary to benefit human health.
- Modern farming and methods of slaughter are inhumane **vs.** farmers provide good nutrition, medical care and shelter for their animals in order to raise healthy stock.
- Meat is a tasty, nutritious essential in human diet **vs.** meat is an unnecessary food which is full of fat and added chemicals, and rain forests are burned and water supplies depleted[8] to raise cattle.
- Zoos are educational and help save endangered species **vs.** zoos are a cruel captivity of wild animals and produce inbred[9] animals.

---

5. **condone** forgive; pardon; overlook
6. **divisive** causing disagreement
7. **inhumane** cruel; brutal; unkind
8. **depleted** used up gradually
9. **inbred** bred by continually mating of individuals of the same or closely related stocks

- Endangered species must be protected by changing the way humans fish, hunt, and develop the land **vs.** human economic growth and development take precedence[10] over the extinction of a few species.
- Hunting is a cruel and unnecessary sport in modern society **vs.** hunting is a regulated activity which thins overpopulated species and provides meat to families.

The question at the heart of these debates is whether animals have rights. Should animals have the same rights as people? Do some animals have more rights than other animals? Should humans change the way they live to accommodate[11] animal rights? These questions will be asked again and again as we continue to share a crowded planet.

---

10. **precedence** priority; higher importance
11. **accommodate** allow for